Camping With Aliens

Camping With Aliens

Don Nordstrom

Dedication

To all the dedicated people, who accomplish superhuman feats every day in working with the developmentally disabled.

I have to mention this before I tell my story to the author. As readers will soon discover, there is no way I should have gone on this trip. But, I want readers to put themselves in my place.

Would they have behaved any differently? Perhaps, but I hope this story changes their thinking as much as it did mine.

Dave

'Here I am, standing in pitch-blackness in the middle of bear country in Yellowstone with four developmentally disabled people. (I was including myself this time in the count.)

We're alone on a trail in the middle of the forest, and I'm solely responsible for their lives. What is wrong with this picture?'

Chapter 1: Departure

'Let's see... eight pairs of socks, four T-shirts, shorts... hmm... what am I missing?' Dave stroked his forty-four-year-old bearded chin with his fingers and thumb as if this would help him remember all the clothes he would need. He then ran his fingers through his thinning Scandinavian hair and massaged the bald spot at the back of his head, hoping that the stimulus would help him think.

'This is the least of my worries', his thoughts continued as he turned and started pacing the floor. Dave was about to go on a camping trip for ten days in the wilds of certain national parks. The trip included an overnight stop in the Badlands of South

Dakota, followed by several days in Yellowstone National Park and the Grand Tetons in Wyoming.

This wasn't what was troubling him, though. His travels had taken him on several outings like this before—even solitary trips—hiking through mountains and wildernesses.

No, what was bothering him this time was that he was taking seven developmentally disabled adults with him!

Adjusting to calling them "developmentally disabled" was new to him also; while growing up, he had arrogantly labeled them "retards." Not that he didn't like people or the disabled… well, maybe it was… but this was shaping up to be an adventurous journey for which he was unprepared.

'How did I get myself into this? What am I going to do when one of the develop-mental's, or whatever… wants to run off and pet the pretty grizzly bear?' His self-inflicted anxiety was spiraling out of control.

Then he recalled how he had got himself talked into this trip. His good friend Rachel had telephoned and invited him to meet for dinner. Her specialty was working with the disabled; in fact, the company she worked for provided vacations and guided tours for the disabled. Apparently, the company was understaffed, so she had recommended Dave.

It was during this friendly dinner meeting that she talked him into going on the trip. He recalled her final plea, "Besides, I need you to back up the trailer for me!" Naturally, his manhood was being tested here, so he consented to accompany her, despite his lack of patience and tolerance for her people.

"Well, it's too late now, smart guy!" Dave muttered as he zipped up his duffel bag and hoisted it up under his arm. With his other hand, he grabbed the strap of his daypack and slung it over his shoulder. His next steps included finding his previously prepared travel cup full of hot coffee and giving his townhouse a once-over. Then he locked the front door, trudged out to his driveway, and tossed the luggage into his pickup truck.

He slid into the driver's seat, waited for the engine to warm up, gazed out the windshield for a few moments, and pondered calling Rachel to inform her he was sick.

Nope, the responsible side of his brain took over, and then he slowly backed out of the driveway.

Dave was to meet Rachel, and the "vacationers" at "Stretching Horizons and Adventures," the company that provided vacations and tours for the mentally and physically challenged. The clients would save whatever money they could—sometimes it took them years—and then pay the company to take them on guided tours or vacations. These guests would simply show up, and Stretching Horizons would take care of everything else, supposedly providing expert staff for safe and fun trips of a lifetime. They would also provide medical care or even a sign language interpreter if required.

It all looked so good and professional in the brochures. Little did any of the clients going on the trip know that the only experience Dave had with the disabled was occasionally umpiring adjusted softball games with Rachel and her groups. The only reason he did it was to help her out, although it took his mind off his pressing business life as a strong-willed business analyst.

He worked in an oppressive environment, sometimes eighty hours per week, for a company that promoted systems management over the value of people. They trained Dave well in not seeing value in people, or even subconsciously within himself.

Now he fended his way through Monday morning rush-hour traffic, and, as a result, running about fifteen minutes late for his rendezvous with Rachel at Stretching Horizons to begin the trip.

Over the past week or so, he had grown more apprehensive as the big day arrived, and now he caught his mind daydreaming in the stop-and-go traffic.

Had he prepared himself enough for this journey of uncertainty? Had he remembered all the necessities he'd need to survive a camping trip in bear country?

He thought so. He'd washed all of his clothes in unscented soap, brought as many unscented toiletries as possible, and reviewed all the material he had on camping with bears. But had the clients prepared, and were they as knowledgeable?

These and similar thoughts were churning in his head as he tried to veer around a machine that was tearing up asphalt and spitting it into a dump truck that was following it. This added anxiety surely didn't help with the months of stress placed on him from his job, which had slowly gained on him over the past few months.

'Man, what will I do if a client runs through the "sprinkler" of Old Faithful, or wants to walk into the "steaming bubbly ground"?' He kept trying to reassure himself that they were Rachel's responsibility since she was an experienced professional.

Then he recalled the past few days when Rachel had spent hours reassuring him he would do fine. "After all," she had said confidently, "the recreational director thinks you do a great job with umpiring the softball groups. Besides, the clients will all be high functioning, and you won't have to do much of anything except teach them your camping skills."

This had somewhat helped him in his decision to go, but deep down inside, he knew the real reason the adjusted softball groups liked him.

"They've got this sixth sense and can peer deep inside your mind structure, and can tell that you are about to have a nervous breakdown from your job, Dave," he remarked aloud.

"You are teetering on the edge—ready to fall into the abyss of the institutionalized, state-sponsored happy place where they live. Perhaps they're just letting you know they will be there to welcome you with broad smiles and open arms, and you will have plenty of friendly company." He caught himself convincingly stating this to the pretend person in the seat next to him.

"I really *do* need this trip," he whispered to the mouth of his travel coffee mug before taking a well-deserved slurp. His mind was truly getting burnt out from work, and the ledge at the edge of the abyss was looking comfortably close. He definitely needed to let nature work on him for a while.

Dave had discovered over the years from his camping adventures that nature had a way of restoring a person back to normal again. He found that the wilderness—especially the mountains—has an uncanny ability to cleanse the soul and get a person's mind right again… putting priorities back in order the way nature intended them to be.

Nature doesn't allow you to administrate, configure, or correctly analyze her creation. Instead, she purges the pollution of society from you by burning, blasting, washing, blowing, and refining your character. Only when she has finished, and you are standing humbly purified before her, does she reveal her wisdom and awesome vistas of beauty, which she has kept hidden just for your personal moment. Eventually, the outside world becomes senseless and unnecessary, with its newspapers, TV, computers, systems, and civilization.

'Man, I really do need time away,' he thought again.

Dave was in the midst of recycling all of his thoughts when he pulled his pickup truck up to the office in front of Stretching Horizons. He noticed that Rachel already had the covered cargo trailer hooked up to an eleven-person passenger van.

There was a small mountain of camping and pack gear stacked up on the curb, and Rachel was grabbing it piece by piece and tossing it into the back of the trailer. She was now forty-five, (a year older than Dave), a wiry five foot four, with hints of gray, smuggled into her shoulder-length brown hair. Her family had a history of heart disease, but, unlike her older brother who had a chest full of stents, she was in great shape.

Dave parked his truck up the block a bit, grabbed his coffee mug and his own gear out of the truck, and locked it up for what would be the next ten days. This wasn't the best of neighborhoods, so he nervously wondered if his whole truck or just parts of it would be there when he got back.

He snuck up behind Rachel and startled her when he spoke. "Need any help?" He threw his duffel bag into the trailer, keeping his backpack slung over his shoulder. Rachel seemed happy to see him, although she greeted him with a strange smile. *'Probably because I'm late,'* he thought.

"Let's go into the office and I'll introduce you to some of the other employees and a few of the clients who are going on the trip," she said while tugging on his arm.

He was at first hesitant, knowing he was stepping out of his comfortable and familiar world into what he could only think of as the insanity of her world. He took a deep breath and tried to shake off his anxiety as she led him into the office.

Chapter 2: Rachel's World

Once inside the entrance doors of the huge, open-design office, Dave looked around and noticed two large desks, one on each side of the room. There were stacks of manila folders and other papers everywhere on the desks, floors, and on top of chest-high file cabinets in the back of the disorganized office.

Behind one desk was an older lady who was on the phone trying to get flight tickets for someone. She smiled at Dave as Rachel said that her name was Carol. She had clown-colored orange hair.

'It's perfect,' he thought, as he remembered Rachel mentioning that she thought a bunch of clowns ran the place.

Rachel stated Carol was the director of trips, and then he met two of Carol's assistants from India whose names he couldn't possibly remember—or spell if he did—and finally four of the seven participants going on the trip.

Ray was the first client he met.

Dave remembered reading Ray's application and remarking to a friend at work that it said, "He gets agitated easily—his application says to give him space when he does." Dave jokingly had remarked, "He'll probably yell at me when I meet him."

Unfortunately, his words were almost prophetic. Rachel introduced Dave to Ray.

"I'm glad to meet you," said Dave, sticking out his hand.

"No, you're not!" Ray shouted back at him.

Ray, age 35, was somewhat hunched over. He was plodding purposefully back and forth while wearing a dreadful scowl on his face. He also had a severe case of overgrown, bushy-black eyebrows that furled over his eyes enhancing the frowned wrinkles on his forehead and the corners of his eyes.

Rachel got Ray's attention again for Dave, but instead of shaking Dave's outstretched hand, Ray ignored it, and, instead, glared eye to eye.

"Well, what time are we leaving, Mr. Dave?" Ray blurted out. Ray sneered through what seemed a now permanent scowl etched on his face. Dave tried to smile back at him.

"I would think pretty soon there, Ray," Dave replied. Ray just harrumphed, turned, and continued with his plodding.

It was at this point that Rachel took Dave aside and reminded him that Ray had some anger issues. She told him to ignore them and make sure he and everyone else on the trip had a good time.

'Oh great,' thought Dave. *'Not only do I have to put up with develop-mentals, but there's one with an attitude. Okay, try to keep your cool Dave… just keep your cool.'*

"Well, why is he even going on the trip if he's going to act like that?" Dave asked Rachel.

"I know," she replied, "I should have personally talked with him as I normally do with all the clients. Things just got so busy that I didn't do it this time. Perhaps this trip won't be a piece of cake after all because I think we're going to have our hands full just with him. I told each client's staff that it was a basic requirement that they are high functioning and work well in a group, but apparently, we have different viewpoints on what is high functioning."

After she explained herself, Dave started thinking that maybe Ray's staff had fictionalized the application just to get rid of him for a while.

"Do you think the staff lied on the application?" Dave asked her.

"Maybe. It wouldn't be the first time, but, not to worry," her voice trailed and got higher.

Not to worry? Now he realized why she'd had the strange smile on her face at the trailer. This trip would not be an easy one. Dave's thoughts were racing again.

The trip agenda stated they were taking these people not only camping but also back-woods hiking. Then they were going to take a white-water rapids trip on the Snake River, plus a hike down a mountain trail. He knew the responsibility involved in doing these activities.

It finally dawned on him he was going to be responsible for these people as much as she was. In addition, he would have to interact with them and actually care for them. His character weaknesses were revealing themselves, and he did not like it one bit.

Rachel was used to taking clients on these types of trips. On one trip, which he could only describe as "extreme adventures with the disabled," she had repelled down the side of a cliff with a securely tied person in a wheelchair next to her.

She had a knack for this type of work, whereas all Dave did in his job was set up systems and then place the right people to serve the system. There was no caring about people or being responsible for them in his job. An acidy-sick feeling grew in his stomach.

Dave was still eyeing up Ray, so Rachel had to nudge him over to the next client. The second vacationer he met was Doris.

"She falls a lot," Rachel quickly quipped, causing Dave to stare back at her in astonishment for a moment.

Doris was a very young-looking age 62. She was sitting on a hard, gray folding chair, and stayed seated while looking up sideways at him through her long dishwater-blond hair. "Hi," she shyly said.

Dave tried to break the ice and stumbled over words for her.

"Are you… um… excited to go on this camping trip?" He wondered for a moment if she would say anything else, but she finally nodded yes with a faint smile and then started talking to herself while playing with her hair.

The third client was Dan. Dave quickly found out that Dan was non-verbal. He carried a large picture book with him he used for communicating. The largest images were a smiley face and a sad face. Dan was quite tall and could have played Mr. Clean, as his head was shiny bald.

Dan stuck a large page from his book in front of Dave's face and pointed to one of the thumbnail pictures on it. It was a sun-colored smiley face.

"Are you happy to be going on this trip?" Dave asked while looking at the picture. Dan grinned from ear to ear while excitedly nodding his bald head up and down, eagerly pointing at the smiley face, and then thumping his T-shirted chest.

The book also provided a picture of a coffee cup, which Rachel stated he often pointed to. Dan wildly shook Dave's hand for a nervous moment or two, then kind of hop-skipped away to a corner to look at his book of pictures and to rock back and forth in a forward and reverse motion.

Most likely, the main reason that Dan moved away to the corner was because the fourth client, Todd, age 36, rudely interrupted the conversation. Instead of shaking hands with Dave, Todd pulled out a checkbook calendar from his back pocket and correctly pointed to today's date.

"This is the day I am leaving on the trip," he remarked.

"Yep—you are correct." Dave smiled.

"Are Mike or Chuck going on the trip?" Todd asked.

"Sorry, I don't know who Mike and Chuck are," replied Dave.

Dave was studying Todd's head. He had a pointed face with a severe overbite. He was unshaven, and he spoke with a soft, wheezy voice. If a caricature artist ever drew him, he thought the image would look like a beaver with glasses on.

Rachel then itemized what to do next and where they were going to pick up the other three vacationers. The first item was to finish loading the trailer and get everyone moved into the van. Then it was off to pick up Gene at the local airport. Later on, they would pick up Mitch at another airport in South Dakota, and finally meet Mary at Yellowstone when they got there.

'Hmm,'... Dave was thinking to himself again. *'That makes seven vacationers, and it's supposed to be a one-to-three ratio of experienced staff to highly functional people. As it is now, it's one staff member to three and a half not-very-functional people—and there's only one experienced staff member! Maybe the next three people will be better.'* He hoped against hope they would be better.

After the introductions were complete, Rachel and Dave went outside to finish loading the gear into the cargo trailer. Todd tagged along and started asking more questions about Mike and what he was doing. Then he asked about Chuck, and then someone else.

"Todd, I told you I don't know who those people are," Dave sternly responded. It didn't matter to Todd.

"Where are we going? Are we sleeping in cabins?" Todd continued asking. "I went camping once with Mike, but I don't like sleeping in tents."

'Whew, no easing into it with this one,' Dave thought, knowing there were ten nights to look forward to sleeping in tents.

After the trailer was loaded, Rachel went over the "med schedule" with Dave. Most of the medications the clients took were to control seizures. None of them had suffered any spells in several years, or at least it was so stipulated in their applications. He wasn't sure why she was telling him about their meds since he was not certified to hand them out. Maybe in case something happened to her. The acidy-sick feeling grew again in his stomach.

By now, the rest of the gang of vacationers had wandered out by the trailer, and Rachel remarked that Dave might as well load them all into the van.

"Well, it's about time!" Ray angrily shouted. Dave and Rachel snuck a weak smile at each other.

After Dave slid the van side door open, Ray climbed in and put his scowling face in the back row. Smiling Dan sat in one of the middle window sections, while wheezy Todd and yapping Doris shared a seat toward the front. Rachel took the driver's seat, verified that Dave had copies of everybody's applications in his pack, smiled again, and then asked him, "Do you want to bail out yet?"

"Not in a million years," he lied.

As the van pulled away from the building and onto the freeway entrance, Dave turned around and took a quick glance toward the back of the van. It appeared that everyone was in a trance looking out the windows—except for Dan, who still held on to his picture book and kept the grin on his face. From the rear, Ray glared back and stuck his tongue out.

'What have I gotten myself into this time?' He was rubbing his eyes, wondering if he should start crying now or later. He was already wishing they could pass through some type of time warp that would make the trip end right now.

The wish quickly vaporized as they sped off down the freeway to pick up the next client, Gene, at the airport.

Chapter 3:
Meeting Gene

All the way to the airport, Todd would lean forward and ask the same questions repeatedly.

"How long are we going to be gone? Are we meeting Mike? Where is Chuck? Are we staying in tents? When are we coming back? When will we eat lunch?"

Then Doris piped in about people at her work. "I like Bob, my boss, but sometimes he makes me wash too many dishes. Yes, Todd, we are sleeping in tents," Doris replied. Todd then started asking her his questions, to Dave's relief.

Rachel turned toward Dave. "See where they are sitting? They will sit in the same spot for the entire trip and talk about the same things."

He looked at her in disbelief. "What the flip did you get me into?" He didn't realize he had snapped back at her until he saw that she had the strange smile on her face again. Then they both shared a nervous laugh. The talkers in the back must've thought they'd lost it—they shut up for a moment.

Rachel put in a tape and asked if anybody liked Bob Dylan. There was a soft refrain of "yeah's," except from Ray who gruffly shouted "No!" She asked him what kind of music he liked and he growled back, "Country Western, but don't play any because I have a headache." She turned Mr. Dylan down for him so as not to bother his headache.

After a while, she put another tape into the deck and cranked the volume up a bit. Dave turned around to see Ray with his fingers in his ears. Dave adjusted the fader to the front speakers. Ray complained for a few more miles about his sensitive ears.

Rachel parked the van and trailer in the handicapped area at the airport.

"I'll be back in a minute, and Dave will keep you entertained while I'm gone," she announced to the group in the van. He was annoyed she assigned him this responsibility without asking, so he smiled back at her with crossed eyes and acted as if he had a bobblehead on his shoulders. She looked back at his immature response, scrunched her eyebrows, and put a frown on her face.

After a few moments of watching her walk into the airport, Dave got his nerve up to turn around and look into the faces in the back of the van. "Does anyone need to go to the bathroom?" he asked. Everyone said no, again, to his relief. "Well, we should stop for a break soon and we can all go then if we have to."

"What are we going to eat?" Ray asked in his demanding voice.

"I'm not sure," Dave replied, "but probably whatever we want within reason."

"I don't like food, except for chocolate, but I will try to eat something," Ray barked back to Dave.

Todd leaned forward again. "Are we going to see Mike pretty soon?"

Dave shook his head no. "Not on this trip. Is Mike a friend of yours?"

"No," Todd replied, and leaned back. Dave scratched his head, wondering why Todd repeatedly asked him the same questions about the same people, whom Dave didn't know.

He then started wondering how Rachel could do this job. He remembered she got involved working with the developmentally disabled after she gave birth to a special needs child. She was no longer married to the child's dad and had raised their son by herself. According to her, it was all from God's hand, and found her passion afterward in working with the disabled. She constantly remarked how sweet she found some of their behavior as she interacted with the groups, and would regale him with stories of the events she experienced.

He thought the funniest one was the time, during a Christmas program at the school, when a group of kids were on stage singing, "Hark the Herald Angels Sing".

One kid in the audience ran up on stage in front of them and started doing the Macarena dance. Or perhaps it was the time when one of the local group homes held a birthday pizza party at a local restaurant. Everyone arrived and impatiently waited forty-five minutes for the birthday boy to show up. When he finally did, he walked around the restaurant, flipping everyone off with his middle finger.

Dave caught himself smirking, and, after a few more reminiscent minutes, he glanced up to see Rachel struggling down the walk with an old tattered suitcase. On the other side of the suitcase was a person who appeared to be a medium-sized pirate from a children's book.

The man was sort of walking sideways, excitedly talking to her while waving his arms around. Dave thought the guy looked like a pirate because he walked hunched over and wore a dark, scraggly beard. Something fuzzed his hair out as if he had just taken off a stocking cap, and had one eye partially shut. Dave quickly surmised that maybe the pirate look-alike shut his eye because it would wander off in its socket, and he closed it so he could focus.

Dave jumped out of the van, ran to Rachel, and took the suitcase from her hand. He could tell by the look of exasperation on her face that things were not any better with this new client.

"This is Gene. I found him blowing kisses to everyone and stroking the hair of the flight attendants. We're going to have to keep our eyes on him."

It was how she said it that gave him an uneasy feeling that this would be the greatest understatement she had ever spoken.

Gene, age 53, glanced over at Dave and greeted him in an excited voice, "Oh, hi—got coffee?" and then he pointed to Rachel announcing, "She's the new girl."

Gene put his arm around her as if he was about to get his picture taken. She politely removed his arm and asked him to get into the van.

They would soon find out that Gene had at least a dozen well-practiced phrases, which he constantly repeated. Gene climbed into the van and sat in the back next to Ray—to Ray's disdain—while Dave loaded his luggage into the trailer. He then realized his foremost responsibilities were going to be loading and unloading cargo and the passengers, and making sure seat belts were buckled up.

With everyone settled in the van again, Rachel turned and faced the group. "Is anyone hungry?"

"I don't like food," Ray shouted back before anyone could answer.

"Oh, yeah, I love food. I eat food all the time, don't you?" Gene excitedly stumbled over his half intelligible words. Rachel chuckled to herself.

"Yes, Gene, I love to eat food too. We will stop to eat in a couple of hours."

Off they went to Sioux Falls to pick up Mitch.

Chapter 4:
Meeting Mitch

Along the way to Sioux Falls, Gene eagerly pointed out cows, towers, streams, corn, and buildings—all with the glee and mostly unintelligible words of a two-year-old. It would only end when he nodded off for a nap. The first pee break came shortly thereafter.

Everyone got out at least to stretch his or her legs at the truck stop/restaurant. Rachel warned Dave that the clients would want to buy stuff at every stop and convenience store along the way.

"If we don't watch their money for them, or keep them occupied with directions or something else, they will spend all of their souvenir money before they get to Yellowstone." Dave would soon find out she was right again.

Rachel started putting gas in the van while Dave showed the people who wanted to go to the restroom where they were. Meanwhile, Gene got in Dave's face, jabbering away at full speed.

"I'm goin' on airpain. My birtday next week. Are you happy?"

Dave was trying to look past him to monitor the others. When Gene spoke, it was with a little Bing Crosby gargled croon, and he always inflected the word at the end of his sentences, making each one sound like a question. He also emphasized the statements with hand gestures and sometimes with serious looks, as if he was stating the most important wisdom of the ages.

"I am trying to see the other people, Gene," Dave finally replied. "Oh, okay," Gene said, somewhat dejectedly. He walked away from Dave and caught the attention of a family sitting in a booth, eating their food.

"Oh, hi,. I'm Gene. I'm goin' on a trip. It's my birtday… goin' on airpain, oh yeah."

The dad looked put out, but the mother of the family smiled and glanced up at him.

"Oh, that's nice. How old are you?"

"Oh sure," Gene spoke up. "I know what you mean. You're pretty and nice."

He shyly turned around, noticed a magazine rack, and grabbed a magazine from it. He stuck his arm out to touch the mom and show the magazine to her when Dave decided he should step in between them.

"Time to get back in the van, Gene, and not bother the nice people while they are eating."

"Okay," he replied, and waved goodbye to the family and everyone else in the restaurant.

"I want this picture," Gene told Dave, and pointed to the magazine cover as they turned to leave the restaurant.

"You don't even know what it is about, do you?" Dave asked.

"Oh, yeah, it's got a pretty girl on it and she will be my friend," Gene tried to convince him.

"Maybe another time, Gene. Besides, you'll probably want to buy something in Yellowstone, won't you?" Gene had a dumb look on his face, so Dave took the moment to take the magazine from him and put it back in the rack.

Todd was the next to want to buy some trinkets. Dave convinced him they had to get back in the van so they could pick up Mitch at the airport. Todd complied with only a couple of questions about Mitch and the airport, but grabbed samples of the free vacation brochures he found in the metal display racks on his way out.

Ray had his typical scowl working as he grumbled under his breath and plodded his way from the restroom and back to the van.

Smiling Dan was unsure what to do. He required promptings at almost every step, excitedly flapping his hands up and down in front of him while giggling to himself. Dave eventually got everyone else moving toward the door and back outside toward the van.

The group got back into their seats again, and Rachel guided the van back out onto the freeway. It was also time for more tapes in the player and descriptions of scenery from Gene. It was entertaining, and the time seemed to go by quickly.

As they were pulling into Sioux Falls, Rachel announced to the group that they would pick up Mitch at the airport, and then go eat lunch. Not a peep came from the back.

"Is anyone hungry?" she asked again. Timidly, and one by one, they said yes. Ray yelled at her for asking him twice.

She stopped at the handicapped spot in front of the airport. "Be back in a minute," she told everyone again.

Eventually, more than a few minutes passed, then over thirty of listening to Ray grumble from the back of the van. Finally, Rachel stormed out through the airport doors by herself. She hurriedly walked up to his side of the van.

"I can't find him," she frustratingly stated, half out of breath.

Dave lifted his daypack and picked through it for Mitch's application, hoping it would have a picture of him. It was missing.

"Hand me my portfolio," she demanded. Her "Portfolio of Vital Statistics" was the folder that had specific details on each person, their medical conditions, and so forth.

"Are you mad at me?" Dave wanted to know.

"No, I am upset with myself because I trusted the company to follow up with the flight plans. I knew I should have called the caregivers back and made sure we had pictures and other stuff we needed."

Her frustration was increasing. "A few days before a trip begins, I phone each client's caregiver to find out about their favorite foods, favorite activities, and any specific needs. All of this information is in the portfolio. The company dropped the ball on the rest of the more important stuff."

She was also irritated that Ray, Dan, and Gene's staff hadn't done a better job of mentioning their peculiarities.

As she was paging through the papers, she was mindlessly remarking that the airline was giving her a hard time, even reluctant to page Mitch. Dave could tell she was getting ticked off.

One thing he knew for certain was that Rachel was the nicest and most patient person you would want to meet, unless she finally got fed up with someone's total incompetence. She could make a steelworker blush with a barrage of verbal thrashings aimed at the unprepared recipient of her wrath—especially if it involved one of her clients.

As Rachel continued thumbing through the information, she was also telling herself out loud, "Not only will the airline be paging Mitch again, but they will also be checking to see if he even got on the plane." She kept going, "Then they'll get security to search for him, and they'll also find his luggage."

After she found the information she was looking for, she slapped the portfolio back into Dave's hands. She started walking away, glanced back with a tight-lipped smile, and then disappeared into the airport once again. She returned through the doors in less than ten minutes with Mitch. Dave envisioned the inside of the airport now looking like Berlin in its post-war shambles.

Dave got out of the van, all the while looking at Mitch. He could tell he was a unique character and took a shine to him immediately—and not just because he was carrying his own gear.

Mitch was about as tall as Rachel. His long, brown hair hung down past the collar of his Hawaiian shirt. He was sporting a Tam hat and a thick beard. His stride was with one good leg and then seemed to force or throw his other leg forward before taking his next step.

As Dave walked up to him, he overheard Mitch speaking excruciatingly slow, and it seemed to take an extraordinary amount of concentrated facial muscle effort for him to talk.

His head appeared swollen and misshapen, as if someone had formed it by pressing one way on the top of his head while forcing his jaw in the other direction.

It took Mitch between thirty seconds and a minute to mouth out each sentence, but his words were well chosen, and the phrases he produced were jewels to be cherished.

Dave thought Mitch cracked a joke when he tried to grab his duffel bag. Dave obligingly smiled, since he was not quite used to Mitch's labored speaking yet. Rachel said something about the airline employees finding him sitting in an area that was not where they had expected him to be.

Mitch literally crawled into the van, introduced himself to the rest of the gang, and grabbed the empty seat in front of Ray and Gene.

As Dave was getting Mitch's gear stowed in the trailer, Rachel asked him if there had been any trouble with the group while she looked for Mitch.

"Not really, except from you-know-who," he replied. He then tried to figure out how many people would sit quietly in a van for forty-five minutes and not utter one complaint—other than Ray.

It was time for lunch, and Rachel was at her shining best. "Everyone will get a chance to pick a place to eat, so who wants to pick first?" she announced to the group. Nobody said anything for a few moments until Todd leaned forward. "Is a hoagie sandwich shop okay? I ate there once with Mike and he let me pick out what I wanted."

"Sure," Rachel replied, "that sounds like a great idea. We'll try to find one."

While she drove around and looked for the restaurant, she started relating to Dave what she had discovered about certain staff and group homes.

"Most of the time, when staff or counselors take their people out to eat—*if* they take them out—they will order the same food for the whole group. Even when they cook at home or at the institution, it is always the same easy-to-fix hot dish or pizza. They don't seem to care about nutrition, so fresh vegetables and fruits are a rarity."

"The clients may not complain, which is probably why nobody said anything in the van while I was in the airport. They are also confined to a daily regimented discipline, although the routines do give their people some comfort in knowing how to do the same things regularly."

She adjusted herself in the seat and smiled at Dave. "I, on the other hand," she continued, "go out of my way to see that everyone has his or her special favorite foods on trips, even fresh fruits and vegetables as you will see tomorrow. Did I tell you about the backcountry canoe trip I went on? I made lasagna from scratch. Oh, and at the end of a mosquito-infested trip down the Missouri river, I surprised everyone with a German chocolate cake baked under hot coals while everyone else was hiding out in their tents to avoid the mosquitoes."

"Okay," she then said, "When we get to the restaurant, this will be a perfect chance for all our campers to have exactly what they want in their sandwiches. I can take care of that part if you will find places for all of them to sit and then help them get to their seats."

"All right then," Dave replied, "I think I can handle that."

"Oh, and, of course, you can have whatever you want also," she smiled again.

"Will you help me pick out my fixings too?" he sarcastically prodded her. She looked away, shaking her head.

"This will not be easy for me, you know," she started again, "because they are going to be shocked that they will get a chance to pick out what they want. It's going to take some extra effort at restaurants to help them choose what they want, although if someone chooses a hamburger place, they'll all probably choose a hamburger and fries."

"There's a sub sandwich place by the truck stop," Dave interrupted, and pointed to the sign. She pulled the van into the lot, taking up almost as many places with the van and trailer as a semi-truck would.

"Okay, I hope everyone is hungry," she said to the group. "Just get in line in the restaurant and I will help you choose what you want."

Dave was waiting for Ray to yell out something, but he didn't, to Dave's surprise. On the way in, Todd asked Doris if she had ever eaten at a restaurant before.

"Of course, Todd," she sounded dismayed. "I said I worked at a restaurant. Didn't you hear me?"

"Oh, yeah. I forgot," Todd said through his nose with an embarrassed chuckle.

In less than fifteen minutes, Rachel and Dave had the group seated and eating their sandwiches, except for Ray, who was picking through his. Everyone else seemed quite happy, especially Dan, who kept pointing at the smiley face in his book.

"This is the best sandwich I ever ate," Gene tried to say through a mouth full of food and then continued, "Oh, oh… cut the tree down—he did it." He then giggled and pointed at Ray.

Rachel and Dave looked at each other, wondering what he meant. They knew he was giving them sound bites of his life and activities, but this one stumped them. She wanted to ask Gene what he meant, but Todd spoke up and everyone else started talking too, so she let it go.

"I wonder if Mike knows about this place?" Todd asked himself.

Doris had to keep moving the hair out of her face so it didn't become part of her sandwich. "It looks kind of like where I work," she informed Todd. "I never got to choose what I want to eat here before. I'm glad you chose this place." Todd beamed his beaver-like teeth at her.

Dan acted as if he was starved, devoured his food and coffee before anyone else, and then pointed to his coffee cup picture for more. Dave grabbed the empty cups and refilled them.

Mitch had the hardest time eating because he had to chew, swallow, and try to breathe at the same time without choking, so he was the last one to finish.

After the lively conversations were over, and when it was time to leave, Gene once again stopped to talk to people on the way out—not only to say hello, but also to ask what each inanimate object was.

Rachel, who was guiding the rest of the group at the front, kept turning around to see what was happening. Dave was doing his best to keep himself between the people and Gene.

"It's okay, he's my buddy," Gene attempted to tell the people while pointing at Dave.

"C'mon, Gene," Rachel yelled and waved when she got his attention.

Gene got excited and said, "Oh, yeah, it's my birtday, gotta go now." Then he stopped, looked at Dave, and asked, "What's the new girl's name?"

"You can ask her when we leave the restaurant," Dave said as he pointed toward the door.

Rachel held the restaurant door open for everyone and then stated to Dave as he and Gene passed by, "I've decided that it's going to be necessary to define boundaries for Gene."

"You think?" Dave smirked back at her.

Now, how to explain and get Gene to comply? This was the new girl's challenge.

Chapter 5: Going to the Badlands

After Dave loaded everyone back into the van, Rachel announced, "It will be a long trip now to the Badlands, but we should get there in time to set up the tents."

"I've got an idea," she said softly to Dave when she finished. "Why don't you see if you can find out some more about the group. You know... ask them to talk about themselves."

"Oh sure, I'll start with Dan," he answered her sarcastically.

"That's not funny," she replied, even though she was smiling. "Okay, fine. I'll do it then."

"Hey, Mitch," she picked as her first victim. "You said you lived in Wisconsin, is that right? Have you gone on other trips?"

Mitch started saying, "Yeah, I've been on quite a few." He then filled part of the travel time by slowly and methodically describing where he had traveled, which was pretty much in every country around the globe.

A few times, Rachel had to ask Gene to listen to Mitch, as he would interrupt him without courtesy. By the time Mitch finished his story, everyone else was taking a nap, so she decided not to bother anybody else. The rest of the way to the Badlands was pretty uneventful.

Dave was quickly getting acclimated to unloading and loading the vacationers at pee breaks, and monitoring them so they wouldn't get lost or into trouble. Meanwhile, Rachel would fill the tank with gas and keep ice in the coolers.

He was even getting better at taking people through the restrooms and back to the van again without them wanting to buy something. Of course, Gene and Dan were insistent about getting coffee, but Dave saw to it that they now drank decaf.

He figured that Gene's staff must have bribed him to do things by offering coffee for good behavior. Every time Rachel or Dave told Gene he did something good he'd reply, "Got coffee?"

The van of weary vacationers arrived at the Badlands camping grounds as Dave and Rachel noticed that a lightning storm was brewing to the west. The group in the back had also noticed it and was getting nervous.

As Rachel exited the van at the park's checkpoint, she looked up at the storm, turned aside to Dave, and whispered, "Try to keep everyone calm while I get the campsite."

The instant she left the van, Todd leaned forward and asked, "Can I tell you something, Dave?" After Dave turned to see what he wanted, Todd started crying uncontrollably on his shoulder. "I don't want to camp in a tent and I'm scared," he sobbed.

Not really sure how to handle a thirty-six-year-old male crying on his shoulder about sleeping in a tent, Dave awkwardly tried to console him.

"It's all right, Todd. Lots of people get scared on their first night camping. But pretty soon they fall asleep, wake up the next day, and find out it wasn't so bad after all and really quite fun. Besides, you'll have company with Ray and Mitch in the tent, so you won't be by yourself."

He thought that took care of it, but when Rachel returned to the van, he started crying all over again on her shoulder. She provided the soothing balm that only a mother can to a scared, homesick boy by putting her arm around him and assuring him everything would be okay.

Dave looked up in time to catch a bolt of lightning strike a rising spire out of the Badlands a few miles west of them. He figured they had about a half-hour to get the tents set up and everyone inside their temporary homes before total darkness set upon the campsite and the storm hit.

It was a difficult scramble to get the tents and gear out with just the flashlights. Rachel and Dave tried to show the new campers how to set up the tents. They ended up doing most of it themselves while the others stared off into the horizon and pointed toward the storm. More extensive tent training would have to come the next night.

Getting all the campers to find their stuff and cleanup was a chore, too, especially with Dan. The others could splash some water on their faces and brush their teeth with little help.

After everyone else finished, Dave stood in the outdoor bathroom with Dan for a long time. Dave used most of the time waiting for him to get off the toilet. No matter how much prompting Dave did, Dan wouldn't get out of the stall.

Finally, when Dan emerged, Dave spent the rest of his time acting as his personal valet. Holding first his towel, then his shirt, then the toiletry bag, then his towel again, and so forth. Dave quickly determined he wasn't cut out to be a personal care assistant (PCA).

When they got back to the campsite, Rachel was offering quick sandwiches for supper because it was so late, but nobody seemed hungry.

After the uncertain newbie campers got settled into their tents and sleeping bags or blankets, Rachel and Dave sat at the picnic table and tried to regroup. They both determined they would need breaks from the turmoil and vowed they would let each other know when they needed one.

After planning out the next day, and figuring out how to deal with the people who required extra personal care, she decided Dan should only do one thing at a time in the bathroom. This meant he could do everything on his own as long as they told him what to do next.

Gene still needed escorting, but she would define boundaries for him the next day—starting with no touching people or talking to them unless they spoke to him first. This would definitely be a giant leap for Gene. Unbeknownst to him, it was called behavior modification.

It started sprinkling, so they said good night to each other, and Dave crawled inside his tent. It had been a long while since the last time he'd slept outdoors in a sleeping bag, and it took him a few minutes to get used to an air mattress as a bed.

He had trouble falling asleep, so he turned on the lamp part of his flashlight. It was his first opportunity to write his thoughts in his journal.

He opened up his daypack and started rereading through the vacationers' applications again. After he reviewed them, he thought it would be fun to write blurbs in his notebook, describing the group members as if they were characters in a play.

Doris: age 62, "Miss Kitty."

He labeled her Miss Kitty because she sometimes took on a distinct personality. Perhaps, if it was a hundred years ago, and under different circumstances, he figured Doris would be a saloon gal. It was just something in the way she sometimes talks and carries herself.

Doris shuffles when she walks, and, if the ground is at all uneven, she stumbles and falls. She picks herself up, brushes herself off, and continues on. Of course, we make sure she's okay, but she tells us in a saloon girl drawl, "Aw, it was nuthin'." I now walk next to her when I can.

She loves to jabber through her hair, which is constantly on her face. Her words involve either the restaurant she works at or her roommates or friends. She isn't sure she likes camping because she "… never done it 'fore." Doris seems to be one of the good ones on the trip.

Ray: age 35, "He hates everything."

If I ever wanted to—keenly develop my critical attitude—I would get Ray to be my mentor. He argues or disagrees with everything we say. The more I try to convince him of something, the madder and louder he gets.

Give him his space. I already wasted too many words on him. He is really getting on my nerves.

Dan: age 51, "The smiling, silent, garbage disposal."

Dan is on the trip of his life. He'd sit and stare out the window of the van forever with that grin on his face, if we'd let him. Whatever we do is a great pleasure for him. He even skips to the restrooms.

We have to watch his money for him though, because he will hand the cashier his whole billfold when paying for coffee or something else at the stops. He also has a voracious appetite— eating everything put in front of him. There won't be any leftovers, I'm sure. It is great seeing his beaming smile all the time.

Todd: age 36, "Wheezy homesick blues."

For some reason, I like Todd a lot, even if he does bug me with the same questions repeatedly. I feel sorry for him because he never should have come on this trip—not that any of the others seemed like prime candidates either.

He bought a phone card so he could call home whenever he gets the first chance. I will take him under my wing to teach him camping skills. Maybe this will help.

Mitch: 42, "Mr. Happy Camper."

Mitch revealed to us during his storytelling in the van that a car ran over his head when he was three, which probably explains why it is so misshapen. He spent ten days in a coma and the doctors told his parents that, if he ever came out of it, he'd be a vegetable.

From that day forward, Mitch displayed miracle after miracle. He confided he is living proof there is a God because He brought him out of the coma so he could show the world, "God exists as the restorer of people through any circumstance."

Later on, as a young adolescent, a car hit him again, breaking his leg in several places. I think this is what forces him to walk, dragging his right leg and then throwing it forward.

Not finished yet, someone shoved him into a shallow pool. The fall broke his jaw and knocked out his teeth, which also contributed to his facial deformity. Consequently, he also has to wear dentures, which is one reason he has so much trouble eating.

However, Mitch graduated from high school, lives independently, holds down a job, travels the world much on his own, and just astounds me with his outlook on life—he is the total opposite of Ray.

Mitch overcomes more obstacles in one day than I think most do in a lifetime. He said it takes him forty-five minutes each day just to put on his belt. So far, he is volunteering to help us out, without a cross word to anyone, although he intimated to me he thought he did a good job of "putting up with Ray".

I am learning a lot from Mitch—especially patience—but it also seems like I am going through some type of transformation, and he is showing me the way. I'd feel like the worst person on earth when he takes a good minute to form a sentence, contorting every nerve and muscle in his face to force out each word, and then I can't understand his last few words. No problem, he just relaxes for a second and starts over again.

Mitch is making me look more like Ray—with me complaining about my simple problems. He is subtly confronting my ideas in how I look at life and people. Am I the developmentally challenged one here in this group?

Mary: age 57, "The Shopper."

We will pick up Mary at Yellowstone. It sounds as if she will be the most functional, and probably doesn't belong along with us crazies. Her app states she is just a little slow, loves to shop and work word puzzles. She will probably do so to ignore the rest of us. It appears from her picture, it will be like having your kindly old grandma along on a trip.

Gene: age 53, "The Funny Predator."

The state institutionalized Gene for forty-two of his fifty-three years. Under those conditions, I guess if it were I, I'd be pretty darned excited at meeting people and seeing cows too. Gene acts as if he has the brain of a two- or three-year-old, and, much like a person of that age, repeats known words and phrases over and over, and finds joy in the simplest of things we take for granted.

So far, he has provided us with hours of laughter, but he needs to learn to keep his hands off of women and not bother people in public. I hope Rachel is able to set those boundaries for him.

End of Monday's journal notes.

Dave turned his light off and tried watching the storm roll in through the tent windows for a few moments. He was convinced they would spend the next day searching the nooks and crannies of the Badlands for half-naked loonies, who ran away at night from the storm. He apologized and corrected himself for thinking they were loonies. "They are developmentally disabled," he mumbled to himself.

The rolling thunder and the light patter of rain were the culprits that finally knocked him out. Luckily, that's all it was... light rain.

Chapter 6: Ten Sleeps Canyon

Dave was the first to arise in the morning and took advantage of the empty stall in the bathroom. He discovered why Dan had taken so long the previous night. The toilet paper rolls were flattened into ovals and installed in such a way that it was very difficult to remove the paper through the fixture. Now he shuddered, wondering if Dan ever figured it out.

Rachel woke up next and started boiling water for coffee on the gas stove provided by Stretching Horizons. The company had also provided tents and sleeping mats for the clients. Dave was glad he had brought an air mattress and thought it was quite cheap for the company to provide only thin cushioned mats for the vacationers.

He sat across from Rachel at the picnic table while stretching out the kinks in his body. He definitely felt too old to be sleeping on the ground. Now he wondered how the vacationers would feel this morning since some were older than he was.

Rachel suddenly spoke up and revealed to him what she discovered about Gene during the night. It seems she got up to go to the bathroom and walked by Gene and Dan's tent. She thought it strange that all the windows and flaps were zipped up tight since it was still about 80 degrees outside.

"I unzipped the tent and found Gene and Dan lying disturbingly close to each other in their underwear," she said with a fixed gaze into his eyes without blinking to avoid looking embarrassed. She then turned and pointed at the tent.

"They steamed the tent up, so I opened up the rest of the air vents. I asked Gene what was going on, and, of course, you know what he said, "It's my birtday, he's my buddy.""

Dave held his head in his hands and didn't know what to say.

"I didn't catch them in any act," she continued, "but my intuition suggested that Gene might have a latent predatory character about him with men as well."

"I can't put Gene in anybody else's tent because Dan is probably the only person big enough to protect himself if he wanted to, and Ray would probably strangle Gene if he tried anything."

Dave was hoping she wouldn't tell him he had to tent with Gene. She didn't, but she determined from that point on, "Gene and Dan will sleep in their sleeping bags at opposite ends of the tent, and, under no circumstances, will they be allowed to have their windows or tent flaps closed at night."

Dave wished he had brought a little brandy for his coffee this morning, and certainly, three fingers of a stiffer shot would seem appropriate for extracting additional comfort later on that night. He went into a type of daze as he clumsily helped Rachel get the picnic tables set up and ready for breakfast.

'What am I doing here?' His thoughts started up again. *'I am not cut out for this.'* He thought he felt some type of panic attack coming on. He took some deep, slow breaths and meditated on what a beautiful day it was with the billowy white clouds blotting a deep blue sky. He then remembered he wasn't working at his god-forsaken job, so perhaps it could be worse. *'One day at a time, Dave. It will soon all be over.'*

By the time they finished setting everything up, the sleepy group awoke to a spread of cereals, juices, fresh blueberries, strawberries, apples, oranges, bananas, yogurt, and cereal-grain bars. Rachel apologized for not making a hot breakfast, but they needed to hit the road. Nobody seemed to mind but were quite astonished at the buffet setting, except for Ray, who stood a distance away, glaring at everyone and refusing to eat anything.

The morning sun was creating strange colors and shadows within the alien spires and rocky crevices that surrounded their campsite in the Badlands. Everyone thought it was kind of funny when Gene pointed to just one of the million spires and, with a mouth half full of cereal, said, "Look at that rock, Ma!" Rachel's name had changed from "new girl" to "Ma" now.

Rachel asked Gene to call her by her name, as everyone else did. Gene tried, but the best that would come out was "Rasshole," which sounded like a different name she definitely did not want to be called! She finally gave up and Gene called her, "new girl," "Ma," or "Mom." Dave was still his "Buddy".

Gene proved to be a constant, most excited questioner. He flailed his arms and pointed in all directions to emphasize his speech and make sure everyone understood how dramatically essential objects were to him. It was as if everything was the most important thing he ever stated.

He would first get your attention and say, "Oh, hi, you okay?" or "Are you happy?" Then it was a non-stop, unordered barrage of questions and statements.

"Going on airpain next Tersday, it's my birtday. Who's dat? What's her name? Got coffee? Go cabin. Cut dat out. Behave. Cut the tree down, he did it. He works on boards. He got to pound the nail—yeah."

These were just some phrases they could decipher. There were many others, but they were not fully understood. Rachel finally got him to settle down a bit and whispered quietly to him.

Gene had a difficult time understanding why people had to have boundaries, but he finally said, "Okay, Ma," to her instructions.

Buddy and Ma spent the next hour or so showing everyone how to roll up their sleeping bags, stow their personal articles, take down tents, and get cleaned up.

After Dave got the gear loaded into the trailer and the campers learned how to police a campsite, they all climbed into the van (same seating arrangement again) and they left for a morning tour of the Badlands. The back of the van was full of oohs and ahhs, except for Ray. Ray mentioned he had been here once before, but it was okay that they visited it again.

Ray took meds twice a day—first thing in the morning, and at 4:00 in the afternoon. Ray wouldn't say much during the day other than grumble or harshly answer a question, which was fine by Rachel and Dave because he could be so argumentative. But it was "stop the world" for him when it was time for his meds. He became relentless with verbal assaults until his meds were down his throat.

During the tour of the Badlands, Buddy and Ma were softly discussing how to get Ray to eat something. Dave pretty much didn't care if the SOB starved. Rachel decided to ask Ray if he would choose the next restaurant—it was nearly lunchtime. When she asked him, they were just outside of Spearfish, South Dakota.

"Ray, would you like to pick out the restaurant for lunch?" Ray didn't answer right away, so she asked him if he had heard her.

"Just a minute!" he angrily blurted back. Then, in a timid, shy voice, he mentioned a particular hamburger restaurant and asked if it would be okay if they went there.

Wow! Had Rachel broken through? Dave was in total shock. Ray was being civil for once. Rachel stammered back, half in shock herself, "Sure, Ray, that place is fine."

Dave looked across the van at her and whispered, "You know there will be hell to pay if the restaurant isn't here."

She just shook her head and stared out at the road ahead, dazed. They both breathed a sigh of relief when they saw the restaurant's food sign at the town's exit ramp.

Everyone—except for Ray—was in good spirits as they piled out of the van at the restaurant. Todd and Doris appeared to like each other and spent a lot of time talking together. Apparently, neither one minded the same old questions or conversation from the other.

Mitch had kept busy snapping pictures of the scenery while traveling through the Badlands. Ray made faces at Gene, and Gene would just laugh and point at him. Dan, of course, was thoroughly enraptured by it all.

Dave didn't think the group had slept too well their first night out in tents, as the gentle rocking of the van had eventually forced most of them to nod off on their way to the restaurant.

Dave corralled everyone in the line-up stalls in the restaurant, and Rachel proceeded to tell the group what the numbered choices were on the displayed menu above their heads. Dave went through the number choices again with Dan until he excitedly shook his head yes to a Number 5—chicken sandwich and fries. After Rachel had everyone's choices down, Dave went out to commandeer some tables.

As he stepped into the main part of the restaurant, something strange happened to him again. It was as if he was moving into another world of slow motion.

As he walked into the center of the restaurant, he envisioned himself entering into a very large crystalline bubble. No… it was more like a wavering in-flux force field beginning to surround him.

When he turned around and looked back at the group, they were encased in the field as well, and the other people in the restaurant could not get inside. He thought it was as if he were waking up into an extra dimension, or a higher level of life.

He realized that the field or bubble had been there all along—he just hadn't been aware of it. The laws of the bubble were being interpreted and the answers were quickly unraveling before him. Whenever he was with people of special needs, he realized that, it was as if he was in the bubble, and the other world he knew was outside of it.

It was a totally different world inside the bubble. He moved along with the group, while the world outside looked in with empathy, amazement, nervousness, standoffishness, or curiosity. They did not understand. They did not know about this place.

Most people outside the bubble thought he was some kind of miracle worker, while others just wanted him to keep "those people" away and out of sight. Now, he realized, it was more— much more. It was the beginning of a transformation for him. He no longer cared what anyone outside the bubble thought.

It was all clear now. The best place in the world to be was inside the bubble with people who trusted him to no limit… with people who loved the fact that he listened, or spent time with them. Ray, of course, was the exception, but, in some strange way, he belonged in the bubble, too.

Then Dave realized some other differences between the inhabitants of the bubble and the outside world. Inside, they weren't controlling or trying to stab him in the back. They found joy and happiness in the simplest of things. Wasn't this the way people were supposed to be? Life's goals should not favor ruling over people or trying to gain power over people; life's goals should be about serving other people. That was the secret to life.

Life was meant to be spent meeting others' needs and helping them reach for their dreams and celebrate each other's accomplishments. He knew now he would actually hate it if someone outside came up and remarked that he was doing a wonderful thing. He realized he was not their emissary, and it was not such a great thing he was doing. It was simple, and anyone could do it—just spend a minute listening to these special people. All they are trying to do, in the best way they know how, is let you know that "it's okay that *you* are different from them".

Dave slowly backed out of his epiphany. He struggled to get back to some sense of reality as he set up the last chair for the tables. The bubble was gone.

'Wow, what was that all about? How can I retain this feeling?', he wondered as he looked up and around and caught Gene's eye across the dining room.

"Oh, hi!" Gene yelled while pointing his paper cup toward Dave and assuring the people in the restaurant that, "It's okay. He's my buddy." Half laughing now, Dave waved at Gene to come over and sit down.

On the way over, Gene continued getting everyone's attention, informing people, "It's okay, he's my buddy." Dave could see Rachel laughing with the cashier while everyone else was standing in line waiting for food. Rachel's boundary work with Gene needed a little more polishing.

After the group was seated at the luncheon tables, they all began to talk to each other in their own way—except for scowling Ray. Apparently, he had not figured out yet that he was a member in the bubble too.

Rachel leaned over the table and noted to Dave, "Their talking to each other is a good sign. As they get acquainted, they will start to watch out for each other more often, taking some pressure off of us." Dave considered it as good news as he was still trying to understand what had just happened.

When they finished and were ready to leave, a gray-haired lady sitting alongside the aisle to the exit set Gene off again by asking if he was having a good time.

"Oh, yeah," he blurted out. "Goin on an airpain next week, it's my birtday, and he's my buddy."

Gene stopped abruptly after he heard Rachel yell, "Gene! Get over here." The sound of her voice broke him out of his auto-phrase mode. Gene sheepishly walked over to Rachel, and she led him outside, scolding him for not following her instructions. "Okay, Ma," was his only reply.

Dave informed Rachel that the woman had initiated the conversation, but it didn't matter.

"If Gene had carried on, he would have started touching her and so forth," she answered back. Dave playfully said, "Okay, Ma," and started pawing at her.

"Cut dat out, behave!" she said swatting back, both of them mimicking Gene.

The rest of the trip into Wyoming went well, with everyone nodding off again, bored with the desert scenery. After a few more hours, they pulled into a gas station/convenience store in Buffalo, Wyoming, the last stop before going through a Bighorn mountain pass and into Ten Sleeps Canyon.

Rachel announced that she didn't want anyone to buy coffee or pop because there wouldn't be a restroom stop for the next few hours. Everyone reluctantly agreed.

Dave unloaded the troops and led them to their respective restrooms. Dan shook his head no when asked if he had to go, so Dave asked him, "Can you stand by the coolers while the others use the bathroom?" Dan looked at the articles in the cooler while waving his hands.

Everyone took his or her turn in the restroom, and Gene was the last to go before Dave could go. When Gene finished, he asked, "Got coffee?" Dave reminded him that Rachel said no one could have coffee because they couldn't stop while going through the mountain pass. Gene engineered a pouting look on his face and asked, "No coffee?"

"Sorry," Dave said. "I need you to go back to the van now without talking to anyone. Can you do that?"

Gene lowered his head as he started walking out with a conned, pouting look. Dave tried to conceal his chuckling as he went into the restroom.

When he came out of the restroom, he observed that everyone had gone back to the van except for Dan, who still stood dutifully looking over the contents of the cooler. Dave reminded him they couldn't get anything to drink, and Dan nodded his head in understanding.

On the way out, Dan stopped by the candy bar display and looked at Dave. Dave said it was okay, so Dan grabbed a crunch bar, got a big grin on his face, and eagerly hopped and skipped up to the cash register.

At that point, Dan handed the candy bar and his billfold over to the female cashier, and stood there shaking his hands excitedly. She looked puzzled. Dave told him to take his billfold back and take out a dollar bill and hand it to the girl.

It was at this time that Dave noticed Gene on the other side of the store, at a different cashier, trying to pay for something. Dave moved over to see what it was when Rachel stormed in the door yelling at him. Uh-oh, Gene was buying coffee. No—worse than that, he thought. Gene had a large souvenir coffee mug and didn't have enough money to pay for it.

Dan paid for his candy bar, and Dave led him back to the van. Rachel stormed out behind them, yelling at Gene to get in the van. Dave knew something else was up. She wouldn't get this upset just because he tried to buy a coffee mug. When she calmed down enough, she relayed what happened.

"Gene must have waited until you went into the restroom. Then he apparently grabbed a large plastic Wyoming coffee travel mug, filled it with coffee, walked out the door, and sat in the back of the van. I was busy keeping up with expense reporting in the front seat and didn't notice any of it."

"The owner of the store came out and informed me that Gene had shoplifted the mug and coffee. I turned around and asked Gene if he had stolen the travel mug. He raised it with a 'cheers' motion, took a drink out of it, and smiled back at me. I could have strangled him."

"Then I spent a few agonizing moments pleading with the store owner, and he finally stated he wouldn't press charges and would let it go if Gene paid for it and apologized. So, I told Gene to go back into the store to pay for it, but he didn't have enough money on him. Luckily, a very nice person behind him in line offered to pay the balance."

Dave had a shocked look on his face and again, didn't know what to say. Rachel was livid, and Gene was going to be in hot water with her for the rest of the day.

They made it through the Bighorn pass and decided to camp at a place just on the other side of the canyon pass. This was a private campsite. The owner was very nice and chatted for awhile.

It was still light outside, so it was much easier to get the gear out of the trailer, and they had more time to set up the tents. Rachel and Dave showed the gang how to connect the tent poles and thread them through the tent sleeves to set up their own tents. Ray's contribution was to hold on to tent stakes until they were needed. He refused to learn anything else. It was even a challenge for him to hold the tent stakes for very long and yelled at everyone to hurry up.

Rachel must have sensed that Dave was losing it with Ray and that they might have a go-round, because she quickly took Dave aside and told him to do his best to ignore him. Dave turned around again and praised everyone else for their tent-building skills.

After they got the tents up and sleeping bags rolled out, Rachel set out to make pocket pita bread sandwiches for supper. When it was convenient on trips, she liked to get the entire group involved with making dinners and cleaning up afterward.

After she got them all to first wash their hands, the timid group chopped up fresh vegetables, pickles, peppers, cheeses, and different selections of sandwich meat. Since these activities were new chores for the group, they required an immense amount of extra time and patience.

However, seeing the look of accomplishment on their faces was well worth it. Ray didn't do or eat anything. Everybody else said it was the best dinner they ever ate, and Dan made sure he ate up any scraps that were left over.

The talk around the table was high-spirited. Dave and the group were amazed at how much they had learned they could do in one day. Todd told Dave he thought camping was fun. Dave smiled back and said he was glad he had come along.

The campground had showers so, once again, Dave got more experience at being a PCA after dinner. He thought it would be a bit easier this time, though, as his transformational experience in the restaurant was still lingering on. He wondered if he should tell Rachel what had happened. But maybe she would think he was going loopy and she'd have to keep an eye on him too.

Dave discovered the men could mostly bathe themselves, but he had to show them the techniques of showering at a campsite shower. Gene had to wait until everyone else was done. Ray refused to shower, but did wash his face and upper body parts in the sink.

After everyone finished cleaning up, Dave sat across from Rachel and Doris at the picnic table. Both of the women had their hair wrapped up in towels from their showers. Doris said she was glad she finally got to clean up. Dave confessed to Rachel he wasn't sure he was cut out to be a PCA.

"I know," Rachel attempted to empathize with him. "You weren't supposed to be doing half of what you are doing." She could tell he was getting worn out—between dealing with Ray and caring for the people who required specific attention.

"Why don't you hang back at the camp while I take the group for a short hike down the wooded trail around the campground," she suggested. Dave smiled and agreed.

While Rachel got everyone together for the hike, Dave went over to a post-and-rail fence and looked out over a field with some pinewoods in the background.

As he had his arms draped over the top rail, he heard some inquisitors behind him, who wondered why Dave wasn't going with them on the hike. Rachel said he had to do something else while they were gone.

What he had to do was wonder: *Was what happened at the restaurant—God trying to show him something? Was the experience merely a trick of the mind or was there something spiritually involved here? Is this what happened to Rachel when she discovered her passion?*

He thought about it for a while, watching as the sun set behind the woods. Then he decided to just let it go for now. There was too much going on that needed his undivided attention. He also knew he'd better find a way to get along with Ray, for everyone's sake.

Rachel brought the hikers back by way of the road they'd driven in on. Doris was shuffling along next to Rachel, and Todd was trying to keep up with them so he could hear what they were talking about. Dan was behind them, looking around with his wide grin, happy with everything he was seeing.

Gene, Ray, and Mitch were bringing up the rear, and Ray marched along the side of the road, keeping to himself. Gene was quiet for a change, while Mitch was taking it all in and appeared quite content to be outside of basic civilization.

When they got the campsite cleaned up and the hikers were all finally tucked into their sleeping bags, Rachel informed Dave what she had discovered about the group and how they didn't want to do anything that was planned. It was during the hike that she determined this group was not capable of handling any backwoods hiking. She also found out that only Mitch was interested in doing the white-water rafting.

It was difficult, but they stayed up late trying to be creative about what they were going to do for nine more days since nobody wanted to do most of the stuff on the itinerary. Dave could tell Rachel was getting frustrated, as she was always gung-ho to show her groups new and challenging things.

Eventually, they were both too beat to think anymore, so they checked on Gene and Dan again before retiring for the night. Dave and Rachel had set up their tents on opposite sides of the campsite, facing each other. That way, they could keep an eye on the rest of the group in case anyone was stirred by wanderlust. They could easily check out any strange noise during the night.

Dave thankfully sank into his air mattress, letting out a huge sigh along with the air shifting in the chambers in his mattress as he re-positioned himself on it.

A horse clopped by once, and then later some sheep baying off in the distance awakened him. He finally dozed off for good, wondering if they were domestic or wild bighorn sheep.

Chapter 7: Road to Yellowstone

Dave was the first to awaken again. He did a quick check on everyone's tent and snuck in a quick shower before the routine chaos began. After he finished, he spent some time at a picnic table filling in the events of the previous day in his journal.

This time, he noted, it surprised him at how quickly everyone was adapting to camping in the outdoors.

It's difficult for Mitch to bend over to put in the stakes or to pick up something because of his bad leg. Once, he lost his balance and toppled over onto his back. He laughed out loud, looking up from the ground with a burst of spastic laughter that caused others to join in the guffawing.

Ray is still an ongoing concern and a disappointment. We constantly ask him for his opinion on things, trying to get him involved, but he just yells back at us to leave him alone. The only time he was nice to anyone was when he got to choose his restaurant. He seems to get along with his tent mates so far, as long as somebody helps him carry his bag. Todd is fulfilling that role for now.

Doris is still in her world of work and the people she works with. Todd likes her and doesn't mind it. I'm glad he got through the first night of camping.

Dan was getting more comfortable in showing his book to the others and pointing at the pictures for them. Sometimes he leans against a tree wearing a tattered hat he brought with him, probably given to him by his staff to keep the sun from burning his bald head.

Occasionally, he peeks out at everyone from under the brim and starts giggling, and then starts wildly shaking his hands after he notices people are looking at him. He is thoroughly enjoying everyone, maybe even Ray.

Gene is on a trip all of his own. What would have happened if the owner had him arrested for stealing the coffee and mug? It might have ended the trip, which now I'm actually starting to enjoy.

After my experience in the restaurant, I am fully seeing how shallow I was with my feelings toward developmentally challenged people. It must be the mountain air causing this change?

End of journal notes.

He wanted to write some more, but the group began stumbling out of the tents. They seemed to be even more cheery that morning, probably from more sleep. They were still in the foothills of the Bighorns, and he knew most people seem to sleep better the higher in altitude they are.

The fruit and cereal choices were prepared again, and the sleepyheads slowly awoke while they ate.

As they were sitting around the picnic tables chowing down the buffet, Dave noticed Gene was especially fired up today. Rachel sat across from him and stared at him in disbelief for a good ten minutes, quietly listening to his non-stop tirade of flinging arms and phrases. He was doing his best to convince her that everything he was saying was the most important subject in the world.

Finally, when he quit for a moment, she looked at him in astonishment and said, "You're crazy, Gene, anyone ever tell you that?"

Dave spit his coffee out on the ground to keep from choking on it in his laughter. He tried unsuccessfully to recall where he had heard that sort of approach in behavior management training. He recovered in time to hear Gene reply, "Oh yeah, you pickin' on me? Cut dat out. Behave. I got Christmas tree at home."

It was the first good laugh of the day for everyone.

Finally, the happy vacationers—except for Ray—had their fill of breakfast. Doris, Todd, and Rachel started cleaning up the mess and putting the leftover items back in the coolers. Dave took the rest of the group and helped them get their sleeping bags and mats rolled up and put in the trailer.

Mitch knew how to take down his and others' tents, so Dave helped Gene and Dan with theirs, and Todd helped Doris when they were finished with the morning chores. Ray stood by a tree and watched Mitch.

After they cleaned up in the showers and got the area picked up, they piled into the van and were on their way to Yellowstone. Ray didn't disappoint anyone with his under-his-breath snide remarks at everyone else.

The road they took out of the canyon dumped them into a dry, sagebrush scene. Gas drilling rigs infested both sides of the road to Yellowstone. Of course, the boredom of the scenery was still interrupted with the same old inquiries from Todd about Mike and Chuck.

Doris had expanded her jabbering to identifying and appreciating the people she spent Thanksgiving with. She also complimented Todd and Mitch for being so helpful in setting up and tearing down her tent, and stated she wanted their help again when they got to Yellowstone.

It was during these times of staring at the desert, as heat rose up in waves from the ground, that strange mirage or visionary daydreams formed for Dave—especially when they found themselves waiting in endless lines because sections of the road had been reduced to a single lane from road construction.

At each site, they had to wait for clearance from flag-women before they could continue on. The lack of any wind didn't help, and then everything mixed together caused Dave's mind to wander off and play tricks on him.

It was probably the commingled remembrance of Gene and the coffee mug, the strange landscape, and the general insanity he had experienced so far with the group that helped trigger a daydream that unfolded in front of him, like a shifting mirage into the desert scenery:

It was sometime back in the gangster days of the Roaring 20s, and he was "Buddy" in the "Ma and Buddy" gang. They were notorious merchant store harassers who operated as what the local newspapers described as "The Misfit Gang from the Loony Bin".

The articles indicated the scenario was always the same. First, "Crazy Gene" would stroll into the store with arms flailing to get everyone's attention. He would walk up to the cashier inquiring, "Got coffee? Goin' on an airpain", and would continue on with his well-practiced auto-phrases.

When the person behind the counter realized she couldn't possibly cope with the situation, she would call out to her co-worker to assist with the arm-flailing questioner of, "What's his name? Cut the tree down, he did it." The problem would finally escalate to the manager.

During one encounter, a security guard, who had just snuck a donut from behind the counter, hiked up his pants and strolled over to take charge.

Meanwhile, "Silent Dan" snuck in and took his position just inside the doorway. He was dressed in a wide-lapelled suit, and the brim of his hat was pulled down over his eyes. He occasionally snuck a peek over his book of faces and pictures, and then knowingly smiled as he scanned the scene happening in front of him.

After all of this had taken place, the rest of the gang barged through the doorway, and "Jaw-Flapping Doris" stumbled in and took center stage. In a droning saloon-gal voice she announced, "All right, y'all, you lissen and you lissen up good! Or I'll bore ya'll to death about the restaurant and the people I work and live with. Now, this heer's Ray an heez got sumpthin' to say too."

"I'm Grumbling Ray, and I'm here for the sole purpose of doing my best to see that you have as bad a day as I try to have every day. I ain't had my meds yet, so you all stop what you're doing and get me some water, pronto!"

In the meantime, "Good Natured Mitch" had taken the security guard hostage, and away from Gene, by making him feel so sorry for him and his lot in life, that the guard guiltily snuck another donut for both of them. The guard was holding back a sack of tears by the time Mitch finished with him.

While Mitch and the guard were eating their donuts, "Ma" untangled all the merchant's employees who had gathered around Gene. She then organized them and asked them to stand in order by the types of food they liked. When they were so arranged, she immediately set boundaries around them.

"Wheezy, Blues-Singing Todd" collected all the freebies the merchant's stands offered. He also stopped by each employee and quizzed them about whether they had seen Mike or Chuck and asked what were they were up to.

When everyone was finished, and the gang members had taken turns at leaving deposits in the restroom, Buddy began rounding them up for departure while whistling the seven dwarfs' theme song.

As a final parting comment, he turned to the manager and said, "You know, there's this new business system out there that I'm sure would help you manage your business better. I used to work with it a while back in another world, and, if you like, and if I ever return from this trip, I might consult with you on it.

But got to run for now. We have to meet Grandma Mary at our hideout campsite in Yellowstone. She's got shopping and word puzzles to do."

After the gang jumped back into the getaway van, it was then that Ma realized Crazy Gene had gone too far and walked out with a toy airplane with the words, "Tersday Birtday" on it.

She took him by the ear, marched him back into the store, and had him apologize. He didn't apologize, but instead, winked and blew kisses at everyone. The "Misfit Gang from the Loony Bin" finally made their getaway and left everyone in amazement with how they could pull off such an event…

* * *

Dave wasn't sure what finally pulled him from his goofy dream stupor, but after what seemed like an eternity of desert boredom and road construction, they finally pulled into Cody, Wyoming.

Whosever turn it was to pick a restaurant picked the same hamburger restaurant chain again. There weren't many other choices conveniently available, so nobody wanted to override the suggestion

The restaurant routine went about the same except that Gene was doing a better job with his boundaries and Ray shouted back at Rachel only once with, "I am!" after she asked him to wait a minute while he was interrupting her orders to the cashier. She was getting as frustrated with Ray as Dave was.

Todd had picked up a free brochure that described Yellowstone, and he wanted Rachel to read the brief summary from it to everyone.

"It says that it was earlier in the century when Yellowstone overlaid the horse trails with asphalt to create the current roads throughout the park, and the park received some federal funding to redo all the roads."

She stopped when a guy with a Stetson cowboy hat on his head overheard her and mentioned, "That's true, and now most of the roads are under construction again and they blocked some off."

This was not good news. as they were behind schedule to meet Mary.

After they finished lunch, everyone piled back into the van, excited to get to Yellowstone. It wasn't much further, and, when they entered the park, the ranger at the station said there were indeed some roads that were completely blocked off and would limit what they could see during their stay. As a result, it would take the rest of the day to drive through Yellowstone and get to the campsite at Bridge Bay.

This didn't seem to bother any of the passengers in the back because it just gave everyone more time during the construction slowdowns and stops to view the scenery.

Rachel pointed out different landmarks and implored everyone to keep their eyes peeled at the mountains and streams for bears. Dave knew this was a "keep 'em busy" comment because the likelihood of seeing a bear in the wild was extremely remote.

The van finally pulled up at the Bridge Bay camping headquarters. Rachel jumped out to arrange the campsite reservations with the rangers.

It was about this same time that Mary spotted the van, and her staff came over to introduce themselves.

Mary was dressed in an all-red rain suit and remarked that it was going to rain today. Dave explained the itinerary with her group leaders and assured them she would have a great time.

After Dave got Mary and her gear loaded, Rachel returned and met with Mary and her leaders, confirming where they would pick her up again.

After they left, she startled Dave with the disappointing news that they had to take two separate campsites, and they were not together.

They had to do some quick planning, and Rachel decided she obviously would not only camp with the women, but also take Gene and Dan. Dave was to camp with Todd, Mitch, and Bad Attitude at the other site. They would do all the cooking at her main site.

While they were driving to the campsites, Rachel asked Dave to give everyone the food and bear lecture. Dave turned around in his seat to face the passengers and everyone's eyes locked in a gaze with him as he explained the rules.

"We need to keep all of our food in the trailer at night. Absolutely, under no circumstances, are we to bring any food whatsoever into our tents. This includes any toiletries such as toothpaste or deodorant.

We also have to make sure all of our garbage is placed in the bear-proof garbage cans, and we have to police the campsite for dropped food scraps. It is also a good idea to sleep in different clothes than the clothes we cook in.

We'll be locking everything up in either the van or trailer each night, so make sure you have flashlights and whatever else you need before you go into your tents at night. Also, do not approach any wild animals no matter how friendly they look. Any questions?"

"Are Mike and Chuck going to be here? Can I meet a park ranger?" Todd asked inquisitively.

Mary mentioned it had rained on and off while she was waiting for them to meet her. Rachel and Dave decided not only to get the tents up and sleeping bags laid out right away, but also get the tarp hung over the campsite picnic tables.

After Rachel found the campsites, and Dave backed the trailer in (fulfilling his true purpose for coming along on the trip), his group gathered up their tents, and even Ray carried some of his own gear down the trail to their site.

Todd and Mitch could now set up their tent with only a couple of promptings. Dave tried to get Ray to help them, but he said he couldn't bend over. Dave asked him how long he'd had his broken back, which sent Ray away grumbling.

Once the tents were up and the sleeping bags rolled out, Dave's group hiked back up to the main site and assisted Rachel with getting the tarp tied to trees over the picnic tables.

When the tarp was successfully hung, the guys admired their handiwork while Rachel went over to the trailer and started unpacking stuff from the coolers for supper.

Gene and Dan, with Doris assisting, were still trying to raise Gene and Dan's tent. Gene did his best to instruct the others about what they should do and shouldn't do. Rachel couldn't resist snapping a picture before Dave went over to lend a hand. It was entertainment at its best.

Everyone, but Ray, helped with getting water, laying out the tablecloths, setting the tables, and so forth. Ray stood next to a tree, grumbling about not eating anything. They all did their best to ignore him, but Dave couldn't resist telling him he was doing a good job of holding the tree up. Mary interrupted and said she couldn't wait to do her "find the word" puzzles.

It turned out to be a good idea to get the tarp up. It rained on and off as they set up camp, and the tarp provided them shelter. Rachel cooked up some chili, and it really hit the spot. The rain had dampened everything, and there was a chill in the air.

It was getting dark by the time it quit raining. They finished with dinner, and got everything washed up and put away.

"Who wants to hike to the amphitheater to hear the ranger talk?" Rachel asked. This required more explanation as to what an amphitheater was, and only Mitch, Todd, and Doris raised their hands.

"Will you take them while I stay here with the others?" Rachel asked Dave with pleading eyes. "Sure," Dave agreed.

"It will probably be late by the time we get back, so you three need to clean up now and put everything we don't need back in the trailer."

"Let's go then," Mitch directed.

"C'mon," Rachel nudged Doris and Mary. "I'll help everyone else with your stuff while Dave gets Mitch and Todd ready."

***

Dave spent the next hour or so seeing that they got cleaned up and all their personal stuff stored back in the trailer or van. The site was next to the well-lit restrooms again so it wasn't a big deal sending everyone off to get cleaned up, or so they thought.

Dave's "ranger talk" trio was finally ready to go. He checked their flashlights to make sure they were working. Then Doris, Todd, and Mitch said goodbye to the rest of the gang and ventured out into pitch darkness on their first great hiking adventure down the road loops to the amphitheater.

They weren't more than thirty yards from camp when Dave's flashlight picked out a man and a woman walking toward them; the man looking very familiar.

"Does this person belong to you?" the unfamiliar female voice asked Dave. His flashlight rose up and illuminated Dan's smiling face.

"He's ours," Dave reluctantly admitted. "Thank you for bringing him back."

"He's not much for conversation," she chuckled. Dave was too upset and didn't get the joke until later.

The trio turned around, with Dan in tow. Dave walked up behind Rachel, who was now entertaining Gene—or vice versa—and tapped her on the shoulder.

"Does this guy belong to you?" Dave asked her while he pointed at Dan. "We ran into a lady down the road and she said Dan walked into their campsite and just stood there."

Rachel had a shocked look on her face for an instant, and then she hung her shaking head without saying a word. Dave patted her on the back and said, "It's okay Ma. It's supposed to be an adventure."

By the look on her face, she knew they had screwed up, and Dave figured she didn't want to hear anymore. Once again, his group said goodbye and started off down the road on their hike to the amphitheater.

The members of the group were so closely following their flashlight-lit circles on the ground, they didn't realize they'd missed a turn onto one of the loop roads to the main road.

Dave quickly asked another couple out for an evening stroll, which way the amphitheater was. It was about fifty yards back. Again, Dave's group doubled back while Mitch cracked a joke about being great adventure scouts.

Doris took the lead, shuffling her feet rapidly. Dave was concerned she might trip and fall, but apparently, she was getting used to this hiking stuff—she stumbled a few times, but didn't fall. After about another quarter-mile, they saw the amphitheater floodlights beckoning them forward.

The open theater was designed in tiers, with weathered landscape ties serving as steps leading down into a large shallow pit. The tiers and benches were set back at different levels facing a semi-circle stage.

They got there before the talk started, and grouped themselves together on one bench in the middle of the pit. There were several families scattered around the theater, but it wasn't more than half full. Although the families were talking to themselves, Dave's group quietly waited for the show to start.

A middle-aged forest ranger gent eventually walked out onto the stage and announced that the talk would be on the Yellowstone forest fire in the late 1980s.

He mesmerized the audience with his talk and the color slides of the enormous fire.

Dave absorbed all the facts the ranger revealed and was truly in shock himself. The most amazing thing he took away from the talk was that, after all the politicians analyzed the actions of the park service in delaying attempts to put out the fire, it had been determined that there had not been enough personnel or equipment in the world to extinguish it. It would take Mother Nature, who had started it, to put it out.

More slides revealed the fresh growth that was taking place, and the rest of the show was on how forest fires actually do more good than harm.

On the way out of the amphitheater, Todd was full of questions about the fire, and Dave figured he had a brand new set of questions that he would continue to ask during the following days. Maybe Dave would get a break now from the Mike and Chuck questions.

Mitch asked Dave to fill him in on a couple of items he had missed. Doris said she liked the show and then continued with her normal jabber.

They made the mile-plus walk back to the campsite without a problem. Everyone else had gone to bed except for Rachel. The clouds had broken up, and she was stretched out on a picnic table bench seat enjoying the quiet and the stars.

The theater group stopped and excitedly whispered to Rachel, telling her all about the hike. Todd gleefully informed her about the fire. Mitch then mentioned he was exhausted, so Rachel got Doris into Mary's tent, and Mitch, Todd, and Dave strolled down the trail to their tents.

Dave held open their tent flap and whispered, "Try not to snore too much because it attracts bears." Ray was already in his sleeping bag, but not asleep yet. He rudely corrected Dave, "No, it doesn't!"

Mitch broke out with loud spastic laughter, and Todd and Dave quickly joined in with him. Ray grumbled to himself and turned away on his side.

After Dave got his group settled in and wished them a good night, he went back up to the main site again and found Rachel upset with herself about Dan wandering off. She was primarily ticked because Dan's staff hadn't sent a PCA with him, because he obviously needed one. It was determined that someone would always have to take him to the restrooms from that point on, no matter what.

"How are you doing?" She wanted to know. "Did you enjoy the hike and the show? Did your group give you any problems?"

"Yeah, it was okay," Dave replied. "The show was good—there were great slides of the fire. We missed one turn hiking down there, but everything else went okay. Todd seemed to be infatuated with the fire and was asking me a bunch of questions about it. I think I can get along with everyone except Ray. He is really getting on my nerves."

She agreed with his assessment about Ray. "He doesn't belong on an outing like this—it isn't fair to the other campers." She then recalled stories of the previous group she had taken camping to the Black Hills. "They were all fired up about camping and hiking and exploring and trying new things."

"That's the way it should be," Dave interrupted. "I think this group—other than Mitch—mainly wants to see the touristy stuff in Yellowstone and the Tetons, and will put up with sleeping in tents in order to do so."

She agreed again with his evaluation, so they discussed and adjusted the trip itinerary to make sure they saw all the things they could see in Yellowstone and would ad-lib once they made it to the Tetons.

"Oh, by the way," she smiled, "while you were gone to the ranger show, the rain that accumulated on the tarp dumped its collection on my tent. We'll have to make some adjustments in the morning."

Dave smiled back at her. "It's too bad Ray wasn't standing underneath it."

They both looked up at the sky, which was now deep and full of stars. Dave started reminiscing about the times he and Rachel had gone camping and canoeing together with their own friends.

Rachel and Dave had been good friends and confidants for at least twenty-five years, and their relationship had always provided a mutual support structure for dealing with the trials of life.

They both came from dysfunctional families, and it was probably this characteristic that secured the anchor to their friendship. On the other hand, after all of those years, they also often found themselves simply smiling and putting up with each other.

After staring at the stars for a long while and recalling some more of their own adventures from the past, both finally determined they had enough for one day.

Dave made his way down to his tent, and was about to crawl inside when Ray stuck his head out and asked if Dave would walk with him to the restroom. Dave was tired, especially tired of Ray.

After Ray crawled out of his tent, Dave pointed to the lights of the restroom, "It's only a short distance up the trail, Ray. You won't get lost—I'll be right here watching you." Ray whined he couldn't make it on his own, so Dave held back his frustration and reluctantly agreed to walk with him.

All the way to and from the restroom, Ray thanked Dave for going along with him and unabashedly displayed his wispy self-esteem. Had Dave finally made a crack in the iceberg with Ray?

When they returned, and Ray settled back into his tent again, Dave finally crawled into his own tent and melted into his sleeping bag and air mattress.

There were owls hooting and either coyotes or wolves howling at each other. The sounds echoed in surround sound over the campsite.

He was hoping Mitch and Todd were still awake to hear it. Not too deep down inside, he hoped the sounds were scaring the living crap out of Ray.

Dave fell asleep trying to remember which had the more crying howls, coyotes or wolves. The corporate world had caused him to forget so much crucial information.

Chapter 8: Adventures in Yellowstone

Dave actually slept in late the next morning. He stumbled up to the campsite to find Rachel and a few others already awake and tending to breakfast.

In his best macho voice, he jokingly asked if his coffee was ready yet. Gene didn't miss a beat and joined in with, "You got coffee?"

Dave had some semi-normal conversation with Mary about where she worked and what her town in Wyoming was like. Did she enjoy camping? How had she slept?

She answered all of his questions with positive remarks and then she asked him if he did word puzzles. He replied he hadn't done any in a long while. She said he could do some if he wanted and informed him she was excited to go shopping.

Todd joined in at the table, and the rest of the conversation revolved around the forest fires and the buying of souvenirs. Rachel assured them both they would be souvenir shopping later that morning as soon as everyone had breakfast and everything was cleaned up.

Ray's application had stipulated that he wouldn't eat any red meat. Rachel and Dave found this to be only slightly humorous, because at the hamburger restaurants, all he ate was hamburger.

But, because of this, Rachel had stocked the coolers with only white meat—pork, turkey, and chicken.

Rachel made scrambled eggs and cooked pork sausages on the side. The aroma was overwhelmingly enticing. Even Ray broke down and said he could eat some eggs, but also determined he should tell her he was Jewish so he couldn't eat pork.

Rachel dropped her cooking utensil and started saying something to Ray between clenched teeth, but then caught herself and quit. It was too early to lose it with him.

Everyone savored the breakfast while Todd told the table about the forest fire talk from the ranger. He had a strange glint in his eyes as he was describing it the best he could.

Gene stared back at Todd and said, "Oh, yeah, fires are bad. Cut the tree down, he did it." And then started laughing while he pointed at Todd. Dave and Rachel were a bit disturbed by Todd's infatuation with the forest fire.

Afterward, they all cleaned up after themselves, and even Ray proved capable and tossed his paper plate and napkin into the garbage bag.

Rachel and Dave helped everyone get their toiletries out of the trailer, and then led them up to the restrooms to clean up.

It was a small circus trying to get the whole group ready to go at the same time. They even managed to dodge the friendly restroom janitor while he was attempting to scrub out the sinks and toilets and mop the floor.

When they all finally got their faces washed, teeth and hair brushed, they wandered back down to the trailer and put everything away again.

After Dave got the trailer unhooked, they all piled into the van and took off—great adventurers that they were—to the nearest tourist trap to buy some souvenirs.

The first stop was about five miles down the main road at Fishing Village. Dave got the group out of the van and they invaded the local trinket store. Rachel asked Dave to help Dan out with whatever he wanted to buy; she would look after the rest of the group.

Smiling Dan and Dave then took off for their section of the store. Dave asked Dan to show him how much money he had in his billfold—$30. Dave didn't know why Dan's staff would send him on a ten-day trip with only $30 for souvenirs and treats. He was beginning to share the frustration Rachel had with these group homes and their staff.

It was definitely going to be a challenge, but he was determined Dan was going to get something he wanted. Dave asked Dan what he wanted to look for, and Dan pointed to a picture of a T-shirt and then a picture of a baseball cap in his book. Dan started looking over the baseball caps while Dave looked at prices of T-shirts.

Things were not looking good for getting Dan both. Dave couldn't find any T-shirts for under $25. He even put on his best-negotiating skills with the saleslady to see if he could get a two-for-one deal. She said her hands were tied because, in a few weeks, everything would be on sale, but for now, they had to get the labeled price.

Dan didn't help matters either because he came over with a baseball cap that cost $19. Dave had to admit he'd picked out a nice hat—one that he would probably have picked out for himself.

Dave considered forking over some cash out of his own pocket, but then, to be fair, he might end up giving the rest of the group cash too.

After leading Dan around for a while and not finding anything else, he finally turned to him and said, "Okay, Dan, here's the deal. It doesn't appear you can get both because everything costs too much money. You can put the hat back and get a T-shirt, or you can get just the hat—or maybe we can find a cheaper hat somewhere else, and then get a T-shirt too."

Dan didn't respond right away, so Dave repeated his plan again, just in case he hadn't understood. Dave finally put it all in yes/no fashion. "Dan, do you want the T-shirt? Yes or no." Dan shook his head no. "Do you want the baseball cap?" Dan shook his head yes.

"That's a good choice, Dan." Dave smiled at him. "And you will have money left over for coffee and candy bars." Dan started shaking his hands with excitement. Dave thought to himself, *'See? These guys can tell what you're thinking. I would have done the same thing.'*

Dan went to a mirror so he could see what he looked like in his new cap and produced the biggest beaming smile yet. After Dan paid for his hat, he and Dave found the other shoppers, who were finishing their shopping, too.

Dan proudly showed everyone his new hat. Dave then asked him if he wanted to go back outside and check out the scenery. He anxiously nodded yes so Dave walked and Dan skipped with him back outside.

One by one, each group member emerged outside and eagerly showed off the cool stuff they had bought.

Todd had purchased a picture book on the Yellowstone fire and several postcards with great scenery. Mary had picked out a couple of sweatshirts, one with a grizzly on the front, and the other with a wolf. She also had bought a couple of pens that had pictures of animals on them that moved when the pens were tilted up and down.

Doris had bought a sweatshirt displaying a Yellowstone landscape. Mitch was wearing a new sweatshirt with a bull elk on the front. Gene hadn't liked anything in the store, and Ray, who had sat down next to Dave, said he didn't want to waste his money on such things.

"Do you have money with you, Ray?" Dave asked, thinking he might be on Ray's good side now. "I'll help you pick out some postcards to mail if you like."

"Yeah, but I wouldn't send anyone anything anyhow," Ray snarled back.

"I'll even help you write them if you want me to," Dave suggested, in case Ray didn't know how to read or write. "Or, it might be nice to keep the postcards for yourself so you can remember your trip… don't you think?" He guessed he had gone too far because Ray blew his stack again.

"No, it's not! Leave me alone!"

"Fine, go stand somewhere and mumble to yourself," Dave said under his breath, but loud enough for Ray to hear.

Ray stood up and glared back at Dave until Rachel stepped in. "It's time to get back in the van," she announced.

The van full of the rookie, souvenir-laden tourists headed off for the Yellowstone Grand Canyon. Along the way, they ran into a herd of bison on the road that had caused traffic to back up for hundreds of yards. Rachel took a side road to see if they could bypass the herd and ran smack dab into the midst of another enormous herd.

Everybody in the back of the van went crazy. They squealed with delight and snapped pictures, remarking how big, furry, and ugly they were. The van literally couldn't move, as it was surrounded by the half-ton beasts in front, on both sides, and behind. "Ma" and "Buddy" just laughed at the ridiculousness of it all.

Eventually, the animals slowly moved away from the van enough so they could gradually move forward to a turnaround spot. Finally, the van could inch its way back through the thinning herd and out to the main road again, where traffic had finally unsnarled itself.

As they were driving toward the canyon, the gang agreed to stop first at Volcanic Basin. It was "steaming bubbly ground," and Dave wasn't quite sure how the group would react. His anxiety was gaining a foothold on him once again.

When they arrived and got out of the van, Rachel led the way toward the site, but for some reason, Gene didn't want to go. Dave wasn't sure if Gene was scared, or just didn't want to go. Dave suggested to him that it was just a short walk and they would be on their way again, but still no go. Finally, Dave got an idea.

"If you go with us, we can get some coffee at lunchtime," Dave suggested. Bingo.

"Okay," Gene said, and clutched Dave's arm, which then made Dave feel even more uncomfortable. Gene didn't at all like the sulfur steaming from the pots in the ground and pointed it out by saying, "Cut the tree down, he did it."

Now what the heck did sulfur steaming from bubbly ground have to do with cutting a tree down, then accusing someone of having done it? *'Gene is certainly an enigma of characters',* Dave thought to himself.

The trail was a boardwalk that stretched out over the bubbling pots, which they slowly walked over. Rachel stopped and read the markers to everyone along the way.

It was while Dave was standing on one boardwalk that his water bottle fell out of his daypack and landed on the mineral-cast ground beneath the boardwalk. Without even thinking, he jumped off the boardwalk and grabbed his bottle, then climbed back up onto the boardwalk.

Rachel was looking at him dumbfounded, as if he was out of his mind when it finally hit him. Here he was, so concerned for the group, and he'd done a really stupid thing like that. What if it hadn't been stable ground where he jumped—like it wasn't all around? He could easily have broken through to the bubbling mass beneath.

He stood for a minute trying to figure out how he could have done such a stupid thing, and immediately said, "Okay, everyone, don't do anything stupid like that!"

"Stupid thing," Doris retorted. Dave was in shock with himself the rest of the way through the basin. They finished the walk and climbed back aboard the van.

The next stop was the canyon, where it was quickly discovered that many other people think Inspiration Point is a great place to view the canyon with its different layers of colored rock. On top was a beautiful cascading waterfall, which was what attracted the horde of visitors.

There were at least 200 parking spaces in the lot, but only one handicapped spot. Earlier, Dave had remarked to Rachel about the absence of handicapped parking in the park. He figured that there were more handicapped spots at one restaurant than in the whole park. She said something about the government not having a problem dictating laws to private businesses, but not being able to regulate themselves. He was seeing it firsthand.

The only open parking spot was at the farthest point in the lot, so she dropped Dave and the group off at the entrance and drove off to park the van.

Some of the gang decided they wanted group pictures taken with the falls in the background—everyone but Ray and Gene, that is. Dave could understand Ray's reaction, but Gene was acting strangely. He wasn't his old fired-up self. In fact, he spent most of the morning pretty quiet by Gene's standards.

Dave mentioned it to Rachel when she joined them again. She said Gene hadn't said anything to her and hadn't said anything while they had been in the store either, other than he didn't want to buy anything.

The group took their pictures and finished walking around the point and viewing the canyon. All the while, Gene hung onto Dave's arm. It felt totally unnatural to Dave to have a guy with his hand slipped through his arm—he felt as if he was out on some kind of weird date.

"Are you feeling okay?" Dave asked Gene.

"I wanna go on airpain," Gene whispered.

"You'll be on the airplane pretty soon," Dave reassured him.

"Pre zoon?"

"Yes, but I think we should get some coffee—what do you think?"

"Okay." Gene perked up.

It was getting to be about lunchtime, so everyone decided it was time to move on.

The group got back into the van and they drove around for about a half-hour, looking for a picnic table. With none to be found, they pulled off the main road and found a grassy clearing where they could spread out a cloth amidst the towering pine trees.

Dave again mentioned to Rachel he thought something was wrong with Gene.

"Gene, are you feeling all right?" Rachel asked. Gene didn't say anything.

"I told him we would get him some coffee," Dave informed her.

"We will get coffee after lunch, okay, Gene?" Rachel asked again.

"Got coffee?" Gene looked up.

"After lunch, Gene," she replied.

Rachel had brought the rest of the pocket pita bread with all the fixings and lemonade to drink. She asked Ray if he wanted to try some, but, again; he didn't like that kind of food or bread. She convinced him it tasted like normal bread. "It just has a pocket to hold stuff in it," she told him.

"I think I will try some without the vegetables. Just some bologna… I can eat that," Ray replied after a moment of thought.

Rachel looked up and smiled at Dave as if to tell him she had Ray eating out of her hand.

'Yeah, and he'll turn on you like a rabid dog in another minute,' Dave answered her in his own mind.

After lunch, the next stop was at another village. Mary ran into a store to do some more quick shopping. Rachel went with her, but her agenda was to find ice cream for everyone. Mary came back with a bag in her hands, but Rachel only had coffee for Gene and Dan. She hadn't found the ice cream.

The group then headed back to camp for a little rest and relaxation. Everyone could use some quiet time to write postcards, relax, or whatever.

When they got back to camp, Gene wandered off to the restrooms, and Dave followed him because he had seen some kids go in there ahead of him. Gene talked to the kids but didn't touch them. Dave reminded him that Rachel didn't want him talking to anyone.

Gene went into a stall, and Dave could tell he had a severe case of diarrhea. He guessed that was why he had been so laid back.

Dave relayed his discovery to Rachel, and she went over his application again to see if she had missed any allergies or anything. She didn't see any and decided to adjust his diet for a while— she'd give him more roughage and only water and a little decaf coffee to drink.

Dave wandered over to a picnic table where Mitch and Todd was sitting, looking over the postcards they'd bought. Mitch wondered aloud what he should write to his family back home. Dave suggested he should tell everyone about this great camping guru named Dave he'd met on the trip, who had taught him everything he knew about camping. That set Mitch off in his special sort of spastic laughter.

After he recovered, Mitch said he had learned about camping from the Boy Scouts. They then shared their Boy Scout stories.

Dave wrote some more in his journal, and caught himself staring at Mitch while he and Todd wrote on their postcards.

Mitch is quite the character, he wrote, dressed in his Tam hat. He's always in a cheerful mood, and, even though he struggles through incredible physical inconveniences, he can provide interesting stories at any moment.

Mitch had called Dave a saint when he'd helped him put his belt on in the morning. Dave decided that, if he ever wanted to become a full-time PCA, he would do it for Mitch without question.

Supper that night was tacos—except for Gene, who had a salad, an apple, and a little skim milk. Ray skipped dinner again.

Rachel suggested they could all go down to the marina, find out if they had ice cream, and eat it while watching the sun go down over Yellowstone Lake. Everyone agreed except Ray.

"I'm not going out on a boat," he declared.

Before Rachel could say anything, he kept on complaining. "I was on a boat once and would never go on another one…"

Rachel then interrupted him, "Well, we are just going down to the marina to find some ice cream, *without* going on a boat," she said, emphasizing "without". Ray then turned away and went back to mumbling to himself.

Once the dinner chores were completed, the group crawled back into the van and headed for the marina. Upon arriving, the misfit gang took over the picnic tables outside the general store while Rachel went inside to find some ice cream.

In the meantime, Todd kept Dave busy with his new questions about the forest fire. Mitch helped out by explaining some answers back to him.

Rachel returned with ice cream bars for everyone.

"Let's go out on the dock to eat them," she suggested.

Now, this was one of the finest docks ever built. It was about twenty feet wide, with sturdy rail fencing on both sides. There were bench seats constructed on both sides, and it opened up to a huge forty-by-forty-foot deck with more seating all around it. A person would purposely have to climb over the fencing to fall in.

Ray announced he wasn't going.

"Why not?" asked Dave.

"I'm afraid of water," Ray indignantly replied.

"Ray, we aren't going in the water," Dave explained, his voice growing more impatient. "You're as safe out there as you are here." Then the exchange started.

"I'm not going," Ray said stubbornly.

"You are part of the group, Ray," Dave informed him.

"I'm not going."

"Yes, you are, Ray. You are part of the group and the group wants to go out on the dock."

"No, I'm not."

"Yes, you are a part of the group and you are going with us."

"No, I'm not!" Ray defiantly shouted back.

Dave lost it. "Ray, you are going out on the dock with us one way or the other—it is your choice how you want to go!"

Ray got up glaring, and Dave thought they were finally going to have their go-round. Thankfully, all Ray did was turn and start plodding toward the dock. Then he looked back and yelled, "You're so bossy!"

"You haven't seen me be bossy yet, Ray, and that's all I'm going to say."

"Well, that's all I'm going to say."

"Good."

"Good."

Ray lumbered out onto the dock, grumbling to himself all the way. Rachel was obviously disgusted with Ray. Mary was concerned over the argument.

"Are they going to fight?" Mary asked Rachel.

"No, don't worry. We've been putting up with Ray and his grouchiness since we started out on this trip," Rachel tried to smile.

Dave was uncomfortable sitting with the group out on the dock. He had let Ray get the best of him. He knew he wasn't supposed to talk to clients that way, and especially not threaten them. It was probably the only time he purposely engaged Todd to ask him the forest fire questions, and Dave gave Todd his fullest attention.

After the sun started setting behind the mountains, Todd asked, "When are we going back?"

Dave told everyone loud enough for Ray to hear, "When Ray decides it is time to go back." *'There, you wimpy control freak,'* he thought to himself, *'see if you can make a simple common sense decision on your own.'*

Ray scowled and got up to leave, while Dave smiled and told everyone, "It must be time to go back."

On the drive back to camp, Rachel asked if anyone wanted to go with Dave to the ranger show again. Mitch, Todd, and Doris all chimed in enthusiastically. She then asked Dave if he wanted to be dropped off or go back to camp and hike back. He absentmindedly said, "Drop us off," which she did when they got to the theatre.

***

As they were walking down the landscaped steps to their seats, Mitch wondered out loud, "How do you get to be a park ranger?"

Dave didn't have a clue, so, after they found places to sit in the amphitheater's pit, he and Mitch walked up to the front and Dave introduced him to a female park ranger.

Dave explained to the woman ranger that Mitch was curious about what was necessary to become a park ranger. She matter-of-factually explained, "Since it is a government job, you would have to fill out a very long application." Dave and Mitch both smirked. "After that, someone would look it over and call you in for an interview."

Mitch asked her if it required any special background or training. She replied that a background in science would help, and also good communication skills.

Dave could feel Mitch wince at the last item, and the ranger suddenly realized the impact of her answer and put her hand over her mouth.

Mitch thanked her, and Dave whirled around, accidentally bumping into Todd, who had come up to stand directly behind him. Dave remembered he wanted to meet a ranger too, so he introduced Todd to the ranger.

"Are you having a good time? What did you like best about Yellowstone?" she inquired.

"The fire …" Todd wheezed with a glinting smile on his face. She looked at him strangely for a moment, then recovered and said that she would talk some more about it that night. She was obviously not aware of the bubble field yet.

They all thanked her for her time and went back and rejoined Doris, who was twirling her hair around her finger. Dave asked if she wanted to meet the ranger, too, but she said no.

79

Dave suggested to Mitch that he could probably get more information about applying for work as a ranger from the Internet, and maybe even find the application there. Mitch said he would look when he got back home, but he didn't sound convincing.

The ranger's talk covered the ecosystem of Yellowstone. Another time, Dave would have enjoyed it. However, his mind was reeling with how to deal with Ray. When Dave got his group back to camp, he would have a heart-to-heart talk with Rachel—primarily to see if they could send Ray back home somehow. He also considered paying Ray's way himself, just so they could all enjoy the rest of the trip without him.

The ranger was about halfway through with her talk when Dave thought of something that sent a thundering shock wave through him. They didn't have their flashlights! He had been so engulfed with the Ray situation he'd forgotten… and Rachel hadn't remembered either. Another tack on his board—Ray was endangering their safety.

After the show was over, Dave calmly asked if anyone had remembered to bring a flashlight. Not a soul had brought one. Then he jokingly said, "Well, here's where Mitch's and my Boy Scout training will come in handy. If we all stick together and help each other out, we will make it back just fine."

Not a problem with them. Right now, Dave was trying to figure out how they would make it down the one-plus miles of road in the pitch dark with turns they hadn't been able to find with flashlights the night before.

He considered for a moment asking the ranger for a ride, but then, he had just finished arguing with Ray for being so wimpy. They would find their way back on their own. After all, Mitch and Dave were on an adventure—and the other two didn't know any better.

After they left the footlights of the amphitheater and were back out on the road, they were surrounded by pitch-black again. It was almost impossible to see their hands in front of their faces.

They waited for a moment to get their eyes adjusted as much as possible to the dark, and then, at least, Dave could finally make out the individual darkened shapes if they didn't get too far away. He told everyone to stay close, hang on to someone, and walk slowly.

Dave led the way, feeling the edge of the road as best he could through his boots. Mitch remarked he thought he remembered a trail along the road that would cut about a half-mile off the walk if they took it. Mitch was right; Dave remembered the same trail, too. Now all they had to do was find it and determine whether to take it.

It was somewhat easy to follow the edge of the road they were on, and Dave figured the edge would curve to the right when they came to the first turn. He could estimate the footage for the next two turns, and then hopefully the restroom lights would light the rest of the way.

No, it was too much guesswork; they would take the shortcut trail if they found it. It would be more difficult to navigate, and they might end up walking off through the woods, but eventually, he hoped they would either bump into a road again or someone else's campsite.

Just as he was calculating all of this, a car went by, and its headlights lit up the shortcut trailhead just down the road about twenty yards away. As soon as the car passed, they couldn't see anything again. So, by sheer estimation and footwork, they soon found what they thought was the start of the trail. Whatever it was, they were going to take it.

Dave estimated the trail to be about a quarter-mile long. He hoped it would take them to the loop road that led back to the campsite. They turned onto the trail.

Dave carefully dragged his feet in front of him, feeling his way along while leading the group behind him. After about fifty feet, he stumbled upon a large log laying across the trail. He carefully stepped over it and helped the rest feel their way over it as well.

He asked them to hang on to each other again and walk in single file. Instead, they stopped and started hugging each other. He could tell they were losing it.

Dave jokingly laughed, "C'mon, guys, this isn't a group love thing. Just grab onto someone's shoulder and keep walking." Mitch started spastically laughing out loud. The sound convinced Dave that all the wild animals were scared away now, so that was one less thing to worry about.

As they were lining themselves up again in single file, Dave caught himself in the moment and looked up at the darkened sky thinking to himself, *'Here I am, standing in pitch-blackness in the middle of bear country in Yellowstone with four developmentally disabled people.'* (Dave was including himself this time in the count.) *'We're standing alone on a trail in the middle of the forest, and I'm solely responsible for their lives. What is wrong with this picture?'*

Dave got the strange feeling up his spine again that some kind of transformation was continuing to work on him. There was no more thought of the corporate world—or even civilization anymore. Just this now moment—this out-of-body-bathed in darkness experience that was somehow individualizing him from everything else. He felt as if he was being singled out for training… getting called up for some big mission later on in life. But for now, he had to focus on getting his people back to camp safely.

He got the train started again, with Mitch hanging onto Dave's shoulder and the rest following in single file. They inched their way down the trail. Dave continued to drag his feet to determine the edges of the trail, and also to find any rocks that someone might trip over. Doris's non-stop jabber, for once, helped calm his nerves.

It didn't seem to take long before they stepped out onto the loop road, which would lead them back to camp. Everyone felt as if they had just conquered Mt. Everest, and they began laughing and patting each other on the back.

As they started out on their trek again, inching their way along the edge of the loop road, Mitch remarked, "Well, I guess we failed the Boy Scouts on that one." Dave thought for a moment but couldn't possibly figure out what he meant. Maybe they shouldn't have walked through the forest in the dark? He had to know. "What do you mean by that?" Dave inquired.

"Be prepared, the Boy Scouts' motto…including flashlights!" Mitch loudly and laboriously retorted. Dave laughed and agreed, and the others laughed out loud too. The restroom lights were soon showing the way back to camp..

Rachel heard the laughter of the approaching hikers. They found her waiting at a picnic table again. She joked with them about their camping and survival abilities after Todd told her they had forgotten the flashlights. She then stated to Dave, "After you walk the guys down to their tents, I have something to talk to you about."

'All right! Surely she wants Ray out of here too,' he thought to himself.

He walked the weary guys down to their campsite, noticed that Ray was already asleep, and then got the rest settled in and wished them a good night.

It was getting chilly out, so Rachel and Dave sat in the van while she revealed she had a talk with Ray to figure him out. "I told him you two should sit down and have a good talk."

Dave interrupted her and agreed by jokingly stating, "Only if I could take Ray for a walk in the woods when we talk." She reminded him of the Vulnerable Adults Act and told him she didn't want to fill out all that extra paperwork.

She continued to describe her talk with Ray and his responses back to her about having him talk with Dave—and she couldn't wait to spit out what Ray had said.

"I can't talk to him! I talk to the animals at the zoo better than I do to him!" That was the emotional release they needed, and both started laughing uncontrollably.

When the two finally got their senses back, she looked through the company policies for evacuating or expelling people from a trip, but discovered there wasn't much ground to stand on. They both agreed again to ignore his outbursts and make sure everyone else had a good time.

Dave wished Rachel a good night, then walked back down to his tent and crawled in to try and go to sleep. His nerves were still a bit on edge, but the good laugh had released a lot of tension, and he started dozing off almost right away.

He hadn't been asleep for too long when he heard Ray rustling out of his tent and mentioning to someone that he had to go to the bathroom. Dave waited for Ray to ask him to go with, but he didn't.

Dave got up and stood outside his tent, with the restroom lights in the far background, to watch Ray go up to the restroom and come back down.

Dave snuck back into his tent when Ray got close to their site. But Ray must have become confused just outside the turn to their campsite, because Dave heard him call his name.

"Sorry, Ray, I'm supposed to ignore you," he whispered to himself. Ray called his name again. "Come on, you pansy," Dave said under his breath. "Use your flashlight and take a chance for once in your life."

Finally, after another moment or two of indecision on Ray's part, Dave heard Ray's footsteps pass by his tent to his own, and he heard him say to his tent mates, "I walked up to the bathroom and back by myself. I almost got lost, but I found my way again without Dave's help. Who needs him, anyway?"

'Oh, if we could only take a walk in them woods, Ray,' Dave thought to himself as he rolled over to go to sleep.

Chapter 9: Old Faithful

The next morning, Dave heard his camp mate's talking in their tent as he started walking up to the main site. He noticed Mary sitting at the picnic table. She looked up at him from her puzzle book and smiled. She was the only other person awake.

He sat down across the table from her, folded his hands, and apologized that she'd had to listen to Ray and him arguing the previous evening. He hoped it hadn't tarnished her vacation. She smiled again and said she was having a good time, anyway.

She was more interested in showing him something and carefully pulled a key chain out of her rain jacket. It still had the tiny price tag on it from one of the stores.

Dave took a closer look and saw that it had a picture of a sitting grizzly with her cub sitting beneath her. The cub was snuggled between her mother's paws looking out underneath her chest at him.

"That is really cute," Dave remarked. "I should get one too."

"Oh, I'll go with you when you want to buy it," Mary eagerly told him.

'Thanks, grandma,' he thought while he smiled reassuringly back at her. She then said she was ready for coffee, so he unpacked the breakfast cooler and got the water pot boiling.

The racket must have woken everyone else, and in a short time, they were all eating a big breakfast with cinnamon-bread

French toast and sausages, with fresh blueberries, raspberries, and syrup—both maple and strawberry. Even Ray had some French toast. It was an incredibly beautiful morning, and Dave found he was quickly forgetting the exchange he'd had with Ray.

When breakfast was over, Rachel and Todd volunteered to do the dishes, while Dave sat across from Gene and Mary at the table. Dave was making sure Gene kept his hands to himself.

Mitch and Dan were sitting next to Dave on his side. Doris was pacing back and forth between them and the dishwashers. Ray was leaning against a tree, scowling and mumbling to himself again.

The table group finished their coffees and hot chocolates while they listened to Mitch tell all about the adventure of their journey home from the amphitheater the previous night.

When Mitch finished with the story, Gene kind of winked at Dave, leaned to one side, and ripped a fart that lasted for at least five seconds non-stop. Mary stood up in disgust and moved away. Funniest thing… it had sounded just like a chain saw. Then, without skipping a beat, Gene pointed at Mitch and shouted, "Cut the tree down—he did it."

The light bulb went off in Dave's head. *'That was it! Cut the tree down means Gene farted! Gene farts like a chain saw and then blames someone else for it.'* Another mystery phrase was solved.

Dave jumped up from the table and ran over to where Rachel and Todd were doing the dishes. He started singing and chanting, "I know something you don't know—nah nah nah nah nah! I know what 'cut the tree down' means, and you don't! Ha ha ha ha ha!"

Rachel looked up at him in disbelief, as she had done so often in the past years of their friendship. Todd thought Dave was pretty funny and was on his back giggling.

"So, what does it mean?" she asked with her head tilted up.

"Gene farts, and it sounds like a chain saw… cut the tree down, you did it!" He blurted back, pointing at her, laughing. She thought for a moment, glanced over at Gene, and, finally getting it, she started laughing hysterically into the dishwater. It was indeed a great morning!

Everyone got cleaned up again, finished the routine of packing everything away, jumped in the van, and started out for Old Faithful.

They took a different route from camp that gave them their first chance to see the actual damage the fire had scorched into the mountains and ravines. All Mitch could say was, "Wow, unbelievable," repeatedly. It was truly devastating on any terms.

Todd excitedly announced that he had pictures of the fire in the book he had bought and that he wanted to buy some more stuff. Doris chimed in and told him not to worry. She would see that he got some more stuff if he would help her take down her tent again. She had definitely found Todd and Mitch very helpful.

As they pulled into the Old Faithful parking lot, Rachel was telling the tale of the battle the firemen fought here to save the lodges. It must have looked like hell itself when they were amid the towering blazes all around them. It was kind of eerie to see an oasis of tall pines and growth in the midst of burned-up devastation as far as the eye could see in every direction.

Rachel reminded everyone to pair up with someone so they wouldn't get lost. The group strolled into the first lodge to find out when the geyser would blow again and found out it was about a forty-five-minute wait. There was plenty of time to take people shopping again, to Mary's delight.

Dan, Ray, and Doris didn't want to shop, so Dave hung out with them in the main lobby. After a few minutes passed, Rachel came out of the store with Gene in hand and asked Dave to watch him as well.

"He was touching women in the store, and I couldn't help the others and watch him at the same time." Gene had the face of a kid who had been caught with his hands in the cookie jar. Dave wondered how someone so entertaining and funny could be a predatory pervert and a coffee mug thief as well.

In order to keep the rest of the group from getting too bored while they waited, Dave pointed out all the cool architecture of the building and talked about how much work it must have taken to build it. Then, after he identified all the stuffed animals mounted around the lodge that they pointed out for him, he could tell boredom was setting in.

Dave noticed that Todd had wandered out of the store and gone over by the lodge entrance area. He found some brochures with pictures and kindly brought them over to the group so they could look at them until Rachel returned.

In a few more minutes, the rest of the shoppers came out one by one, and then "Ma" took Gene back into the store so he could buy what he wanted. The others showed off all the new stuff they had bought.

Todd had bought a VCR tape about the fire, and Mitch had picked out a handmade leather wallet. Mary had bought some more pens and a token plastic ring. She gave one pen to Dave and said it was his present for taking her on the trip, and that the ring was for Rachel.

He tried to tell her they couldn't accept the gifts, but she was insistent and had a hurt look on her face. He finally agreed, thanked her for the pen, and claimed that the ring meant that Mary and Rachel were now Old Faithful sisters—to Mary's beaming smile.

Rachel finally returned with Gene, who had found a Smokey the Bear teddy bear he'd wanted.

'What is it with Gene?' Dave was trying to figure him out again. *'Or is he just a con man in disguise? Does he hide within*

his retarded and cute childlikeness so he can get away with stealing coffee mugs and groping women... or maybe even tent mates?'

Rachel also unsuccessfully tried to tell Mary they couldn't take the gifts. She also thought that Old Faithful sisterhood was great and would never forget it.

Everyone gathered together again outside the lodge and began the stroll out across the boardwalks toward the seating area, where they could wait for Old Faithful to blow her gusher. Todd tried to take Ray's hand, and Ray yanked it away and scowled at him.

"You don't have to hold onto anyone's hand, Ray, just don't wander off," Dave advised.

"I won't, but I don't like to be touched," Ray growled back.

Todd and Mitch then became a pair while Gene grabbed onto the arm of "Buddy" again, and they all followed the three women to the site. Dave spent some extra time trying to explain to Gene where they were going and what they would see.

The gang finally all found seats, sitting in a line in the back row of the bleachers. A group of eight- to ten-year-old boys was sitting on the long bench in front of them.

Everyone was sitting quietly watching the mounded Old Faithful letting out her normal, small, vaporous amount of steam. It was then that Gene decided it was a good time to let out some steam, as well. He fired up the chain saw and cut the tree down again for another good 5 seconds. The sound loudly reverberated off of the metal benches they were sitting on.

All the kids in front of him started giggling and turning around, pointing at Gene and laughing. Gene started giggling with them, accusing and pointing at one of the kids. "He did it! He cut the tree down." Of course, they all laughed even harder, and the boys started pointing at each other, claiming, "he did it."

This sent Gene rolling backwards, laughing and holding his fingers over his nose and pointing at different boys claiming each had cut the tree down.

Dave had to get up to walk around because he was laughing so hard. He finally wandered down to where Rachel was sitting. She was at the far end of the line but figured out what had happened, and Dave confirmed it for her. Soon, she was bent over laughing, too.

After they calmed down again, Rachel mentioned to Dave that he could take some time out to tour the other lodge if he wanted to. She knew he enjoyed looking at unique architecture, so he took advantage of her offer and walked down to wander through the other lodge. It was even more impressive than the first.

He walked out onto the second-story deck in time to watch the faithful one gush out her steam. It didn't last too long, and he figured it was time to get back.

The group walked around some more, looked at another geyser, then left to find a picnic table where they could eat their lunch.

They drove to the outer parking lot and found a cleared picnic area setting in some pine trees. Even Ray said he would eat a sandwich. Dave noticed the little smile on Rachel's face again—another minor victory for her.

It was well known now that Mitch had an obstacle to overcome whenever he was eating. He would have to focus on his breathing and then time his chewing and swallowing perfectly; otherwise, he would choke. He choked almost at every meal.

Ray was now, surprisingly, sitting at the end of the table with the group, quietly eating his sandwich. It was the first time he had ever sat down to eat lunch with the group.

Mitch was standing over him at the end of the table. It was during this time that Mitch had a mouth full of chewed-up sandwich and misfired on his breathing. He choked and then blew a huge mouthful of his sandwich chunks on the table in front of Ray—and on Ray's sandwich and plate. Ray's thick eyebrows were dripping with chunks also.

Mitch quickly reacted and jerked, trying to wipe the mess off the table, attempting to say he was sorry. Then he topped off the event by spilling his punch on Ray at the same time.

Dave had to get up and walk around again so no one could see him howling with laughter. Vengeance might be the Lord's, but Dave was reveling in sweet, revengeful laughter. In one fell swoop, Mitch had done to Ray what Dave had been hoping he could do all along—bring him down a few notches. Rachel tried to hide her smile as she shook her head at Dave's juvenile reactions.

Ray sat there wiping himself off, stupefied that anyone could do such a thing to him. Here he had finally broken down enough to sit down and be part of the group, and Mitch had spewed his food and drink on him. Ray didn't know what to say, so he didn't.

Dave resolved at that moment the next time he started getting angry with Ray, all he had to do was replay that scene again in his mind, and Ray's argumentative rants would dissolve in an instant.

After lunch, everyone loaded up in the van to do some more sightseeing. It was then that Mary again proved her value by pointing out some elk she spotted in the woods by the road.

Dave jumped out of the van and snuck up on them with everyone's cameras stashed in his pockets to take pictures. He enjoyed doing it until it started clouding up and then raining hard. After that, the game got old in a hurry.

***

The rain stopped by the time they pulled into Gibbons Falls, where they took some more pictures, and then drove into another village.

Rachel and Mary went off to find some ice cream bars, while Dave led the rest of the gang to a sheltered area. The sun came back out, and it was beautiful again with the glistening raindrops clinging onto the pine needles and the fresh smell of pine everywhere.

When the women returned, Mary asked Dave if he wanted to go shopping with her while everyone else ate their bars. Rachel thought it was a good idea, and he went down to the store with her so she could help him find a key chain like hers with the mother grizzly and her cub.

There were hundreds of key chains, so it took them a while to find the one they were looking for. After she spotted it and gave it to him, she also found a poster with the same picture of the grizzlies on it, and that ended up in his checkout bag as well. She was glad she had found the gifts for him.

When they got back to the group, Dave proudly showed off what he had bought, while Mary brightly smiled at him. They all finished their ice cream bars and left again to go back to camp.

Since everything was damp from all the rain, and they would have to break camp early the next morning before they left for the Tetons, Rachel said she would take everyone up to the lodge for their supper. Mainly, it would be a well-deserved break for her.

Todd and Dave hiked down to the main ranger station so Todd could call home with his phone card. In the meantime, the gang puttered around camp for a few hours before leaving for the lodge.

Todd wanted Dave to talk to his dad, but Dave told him he was the one who had wanted to call, so he said, "Talk to your own dad."

After a while, Todd again stuck the phone in Dave's face and told him to say "hi" to his dad. Dave reluctantly spoke into the phone. Todd's dad wanted to know who was paying for the call, and Dave explained the phone card to him. He also wanted to know why Todd was calling, and Dave again explained that he thought he was a little homesick. His dad thought that was funny. Dave didn't.

Dave gave the phone back to Todd, who said a few more words to his dad. Then they hiked their way back to camp. All along the way, Todd asked his questions again about the fire. When they returned, it was time to go to the lodge at Fishing Village for supper.

It was a cafeteria-style set up in the lodge, and Rachel figured it would be easier if they sat everyone down first, took their orders, and went up to get the food for them. Mary and—yes, believe it or not—Ray volunteered to help get the food and bring it back to the table. Of course, when Ray got his own food, he forgot about helping the others.

It all went extremely smoothly, and everyone had a good time stuffing themselves.

Afterward, they wandered out onto the huge front porch to sit and digest their meal while quietly staring out over Yellowstone Lake and the mountains in the background. They all sat there for a long while like a bunch of fattened grizzlies getting ready for a long winter's hibernation.

On the way back to camp, Rachel found out that everyone decided this time to go to the amphitheater, so they stopped in to watch the show.

"How are you going to keep Gene quiet for an hour during the show?" Dave asked Rachel.

"You don't think I can? Not a problem… watch me," she challenged him.

The misfit gang of campers took up a row in the center of the pit while a park ranger was working the audience to find out who had come the farthest to see the show. Another park ranger then showed up and the first ranger told everyone it was the newcomer's fiftieth birthday and asked if they would all sing happy birthday to him.

Dave could see Rachel sweating. Gene was getting excited—very excited. He whispered repeatedly to "Ma." He tried to stand up, and he pointed repeatedly at the stage. Rachel somehow worked her magic, and the only sound Gene made through the song was at the very end when he added his own loud, "Hey!" The audience thought it was a fitting end and clapped their approval.

The show was on grizzly bears, and everyone was captivated by the presentation. The ranger reinforced what Dave had been saying all along about keeping food and scraps picked up and other bear-safe practices.

After the birthday song, Gene never said another word throughout the show. The group seemed to change after that night. They were becoming seasoned campers. It didn't take as many promptings to get them to help out or volunteer. This was by far the best day yet. Too bad it was their last in Yellowstone.

Chapter 10: Grand Tetons

Dave slept in later than usual again. Rachel had been up for a while and had the water boiling for coffee. The rest of the group in the main camp were beginning to rouse out of their tents.

Rachel and Dave stood over the gas stove to catch a few heat rays to fend off the morning chill. He teased Rachel about how he supposed she thought she was the miracle worker for keeping Gene quiet during the show. She just smiled proudly after remarking that it had been such "a piece of cake."

Gene came over after he heard his name mentioned, so she asked him to get her some water for the dishes.

"Okay, Ma," he said joyfully. As Gene was walking with the bucket up by the restrooms to the faucet, he suddenly noticed a woman standing over the spigot. The woman looked up and said good morning to him. Gene stopped in his tracks, turned around, and yelled, "Ma!"

The woman got embarrassed. She yelled back that she was sorry and backed away from the fountain. Rachel started laughing and told him it was okay. Dave went up and explained to the woman that they were trying to get him to quit talking to strangers. After Gene talked to her for a while, she understood why. Rachel was still smiling when they returned. She so enjoyed her work.

Since they had to tear down camp and get to the Tetons, it was the cereal breakfast buffet again this morning. The group was getting used to having such luxuries while camping.

Everyone was getting the hang of camping now and needed only a couple of suggestions for getting tents down and gear stowed. Ray coerced Todd into rolling up his sleeping bag for him because he still didn't know how.

Gene had a "stuff sack" for his sleeping bag, and he just couldn't quite figure out this time how to get everything stuffed back into the sack. He told Dave that Dave was doing it wrong when he tried to help, so Dave let him struggle with it for a while longer before Gene asked him to come back and help again.

It was discovered on the trip that after Gene learned how to do something one way; he refused to learn any alternative ways. If they were on hard ground, for example, Dave would tell Gene it wasn't necessary to get the tent stakes all the way in the ground. However, Dave would come back in fifteen minutes to find Gene still trying to get a stake all the way in. After Gene had the thing bent in three different directions and barely in the ground, he would excitedly show Dave, "I did it"!

With all of the gear and gang now loaded and the trailer hooked up, Dave and Rachel jumped into the van to take off for the Tetons. There was only one problem—a dead battery. Dave walked down to the next campsite to see if anyone could give them a jump.

"Not a problem," an elderly soul replied.

The guy had a few teeth missing, so, when he spoke, every time he uttered an s, he would whistle.

The gang in back of the van had their necks stretched to watch the battery-jumping event. After the guy drove his car up to the van, he noticed them and asked, "You folk's (whistle) social (whistle) workers (whistle) or something (whistle)?"

"Nah," Dave replied, "we're just taking some special people out camping." He pretended to scratch his nose so the man wouldn't see him smiling.

They already had jumper cables in the van, so all the kindly gent had to do was open his hood and let Dave hook up the cables. The van popped right off, and the guy refused the $5 that Dave offered him. Dave thanked him and then they started down the loop roads while everyone else waved thanks to the nice man.

The first stop was at Grant Village on the way to the Tetons. This was where they were supposed to drop off Mary when it was time to go back home. Rachel wanted to make sure they knew where the lodge was so they didn't have to lollygag around trying to find the group that would take her home again. It also gave them a chance to check their phone messages back home.

Dave had only one work-related message, which he forwarded to another person. Rachel had a worse message. Her brother had had a heart attack and was in intensive care. She tried to call him but, for some strange reason, her phone card quit working.

When she returned to the van, she was visibly upset. Ray had been grumbling out loud all the while she was gone. He was mad because she was taking too long. Dave was doing his best not to lose it again with him.

Dave tried to get his cell phone to work for her, but the mountains blocked reception. An eerie silence overcame the van all the way down the roads into Colter Bay.

Dave tried his cell phone again at this point and it sort of worked. He thought he had got the phone number of the hospital her brother was in from information, but when Rachel called the number, it was the wrong one. Then the phone quit again. The frustration was building faster than the rain clouds that were also forming.

After they got to their new campsite, Rachel took off in the van to buy another phone card. Everyone else set up camp again. It was raining, but they somehow kept everything mostly dry.

Rachel returned to say that she had talked with her brother, and he was home feeling much better. It was obvious that a load the size of the Teton mountain range had been removed from her shoulders.

After they finished setting up camp, they decided to drive into Jackson Hole to have a late lunch and do some sightseeing.

There was more road construction to put up with in the Tetons, so it took a couple of hours to get to Jackson Hole. They also crossed the Snake River twice and remarked at how low it was considering all the rain.

When they finally arrived, Mitch picked another hamburger spot as his choice of restaurant, so most had burgers "their" way, while the rest had chicken sandwiches.

After lunch, they drove into Teton Village, which is a skiing mecca in the winter. There is also a tram that carries passengers about 10,000 feet to the top of Rendezvous Mountain, which Dave thought was only a few thousand feet shorter than the Grand Teton mountain. Rachel was hoping she could get everyone to go up it in the tram, but, again, only Mitch, Todd, and Doris wanted to go.

Dave and his three amigos climbed aboard the tram and waved goodbye to the rest of the group on the ground as the tram took off up the mountain. Rachel would take everyone else on a sightseeing hike through Teton village while they were gone.

Dave had climbed to the top of a mountain in Colorado once that was pretty high, but he didn't think it had been this high.

The tram dropped the group off at the very top, where the land formed a small plateau. Looking toward what seemed to him to be north, he saw only a ravine and another small mountain between them and Grand Teton Mountain. It appeared as though they were just as high as it was, even if they weren't. In fact, it seemed as if they were on the highest point around because they were actually looking down on other mountains.

Dave was getting quite anxious again while they were up there—not because of the height, but because all there was for security was a rope around the edges of the plateau. The land then sheered off for hundreds of feet, and the footing wasn't that great next to the rope. Both Mitch and Doris had proven many times before that they were not the most graceful of walkers. Dave did his best to keep them toward the center of the area and away from the edges.

The group took some great pictures as they marveled at the scenery. It was also quite chilly as they looked down into the patches of snow and ice, and they could tell it was still raining back at Colter Bay and their campsite. Dave also saw parts of the trail that zigzagged all the way back down. The itinerary said they could hike part of that trail down and back to the village. It would have been fun to do that, but the group had already admitted they were not that adventurous.

When about an hour passed, the explorers on top of the world decided they had seen enough of their new discovery, and took the next tram back down the mountain.

***

They found Rachel leading the rest of the troops around the storefronts of the village. After she listened to the excitement from the explorers, she mentioned she had found a great place for a group picture. Ray gruffly argued that he didn't want his picture taken—as if anyone cared anymore.

The place she had found was a long bench in front of a lodge. Someone had carved bear cubs out of wood and placed them at different spots along the bench. There was another larger bear carving standing on its hind haunches behind the bench.

Rachel took a group picture first, as people posed with their arms around the cubs. Then the picture-snapping gleefully commenced, with everyone taking turns on the bench.

Inside the lodge was a huge stuffed bison, and most everyone also wanted a picture of themselves standing in front of the beast. Todd and Doris were a bit overwhelmed by how big it was, and didn't take their eyes off of it during the shot.

Once the picture taking was over, the group piled into the van and made their way back to camp.

It was still raining, and the ground was soaked. Not everyone had brought rain gear, so the ones who didn't were forced to either sit in the van, which was Ray's choice or underneath the tarp at the picnic tables.

The plan for the evening had been to roast hot dogs over a campfire, but everyone was disappointed because it was raining. They thought it was impossible to build a fire. Dave told them they would still do it, but they didn't believe him when he told them there was dry wood everywhere around them.

He told them to look around and tell him where they thought he would find the dry wood. After some long thought, some said under the logs. Mitch said under the pine trees. Dave said Mitch was correct.

Mitch had noticed all the dead branches that always accumulate at the bottom of pine trees, and the mystery was solved.

But just to make sure, Rachel and Todd went up to the ranger station to buy some dry wood. The trip there was also an opportunity for Todd to call home again. By the time they got back, Dave had a crackling fire going, but they stacked some of their dry logs on top of it just to make everyone happy.

It quit raining long enough for everyone to come out from underneath the tarp to roast hot dogs. Ray eventually came out of the van and told Rachel to cook his dog because he was afraid of fire.

"I will, Ray, but you will have to wait until I am finished with helping everyone else." He got mad and told her he wouldn't wait. She finally lost it with him—not as seriously as Dave had the other night, but she argued with him long enough to get him yelling pretty good. She thought he was going to get violent with her, so she backed off. Dave prayed for him to try, but then he interrupted the argument and offered to cook Ray's "freaking hot dog" for him.

For some strange reason, Dave forgot about that dog and, after about fifteen minutes, it wasn't quite cinders, but it was definitely well done. Dave noticed Crabby take it from the fire and eat the whole thing without saying a word. So much for Ray being afraid of fire.

While they all munched on their food, Dave asked if they knew where their flashlights were because it was going to be dark soon. Ray told Dave to walk up to his tent to get his because it was too dark for him. Dave told him it wasn't dark yet, and Ray argued back that it was. Dave sternly looked at him and said, "If you want it, go get it." Ray glared back, but got up to walk to his tent.

Dave went over to the van where Rachel was now cooling off from her event with Ray. She was trying to organize all the souvenirs and trinkets. He asked her if she really thought it would cause too much paperwork if he were to straighten out Ray in the woods. She didn't think so anymore.

Todd strolled over and said he would take Ray to the tent when they all went to bed later on. Rachel gave him a big hug, causing him to produce a shy smile and a beet-red face.

Gene then came by and stopped the conversation, stating that he wanted to go to the bathroom and get some water to drink. Dave suggested he would go with him, since there were scouts camping just down the road.

Dave and Gene hiked up to the restrooms where the drinking fountain and water faucet were. Gene tried to get a drink out of the fountain, but it was broken. Dave asked him to hand him his water bottle and he filled it from the faucet.

Gene thought the water smelled a little funny and yelled, "Poison"! No matter what Dave told him, Gene was convinced the water was poisoned and refused to drink it. Finally, Dave led him around the fountain and pointed to the faucet.

"See, Gene, it's from the pipe. Just like the pipe at Yellowstone where you got water before."

Gene thoughtfully considered what Dave said for a moment and asked, "From the pipe?"

"Yes, just like the Yellowstone pipe." Then it was as if Gene had discovered gold. He started laughing and repeating, "From the pipe, from the pipe?"

Dave kept replying, "Yes, from the pipe." Then Gene suddenly stopped his antics, got a look of serious understanding on his face, and stated, "Ah… from the pipe, it's okay… water from the pipe."

Then he stopped again, looked up, got a serene look on his face this time, folded his hands, and started singing the Country Western song about cool water. Dave had to hold onto the fountain with both hands for support he was laughing so hard.

Dave was still chuckling while Gene went to the bathroom. Finally, they wandered back down to the campsite. Gene spotted Rachel and convinced her the water wasn't poisoned because it came from the pipe. She first gave him a strange look, then looked at Dave until he explained the ordeal to her while he was trying to catch his breath between his still uncontrolled laughing. It immediately put her in a better mood.

Everyone gathered together under the tarp again to avoid the rain for the rest of the evening, as they watched the fire and listened to Doris and Gene trade off on their jabbering. Gene finally said he was tired, so Rachel led him up to his tent to go to sleep.

After she returned, she asked everyone, one by one, what had been his or her favorite part so far on the trip. Dan excitedly nodded yes to "everything".

Doris liked the bison; Mitch liked the tram and the ranger talks. Todd enjoyed seeing the stuff about the fire, and Ray snorted- he didn't like anything.

Mary thought seeing the elks and the bison was her favorite. Dave wanted to say his favorite was Mitch spewing his food and drink on Ray, but changed it to the walk back from the amphitheater in the dark, at which Mitch started spastically laughing again. Rachel said she liked the mountains and looking at all the stars.

After a few moments of silence, Doris started talking about her roommates and the people at work again, and Todd told her about the fire.

The group was thoughtfully watching the embers flare up now and then when, suddenly, Gene started yelling from his tent in the woods. Rachel and Dave ran up to see what was the matter.

They hurriedly flung the tent flaps open to find Gene all tangled up in his sleeping bag, pointing and swearing at his shoes. They figured he'd had a bad dream in which his shoes started attacking him or something. Then a chipmunk stuck his head out of one of Gene's tennis shoes. Gene started screaming as Dave grabbed the shoe and took it outside to shake out the varmint.

Rachel got him calmed down, untangled, and back in order while he acted like a little kid letting "Ma" tuck him in at night. After that event, they went back down to the fire and told everyone else it was time to hit the hay. The term "hit the hay" turned out to be something funny to the group, and they looked at each other, laughing.

Dave liked this campsite a lot better than the one at Yellowstone. It was much more remote and deeper in the woods. It continued to rain lightly that night. Dave slept the best yet with the rain tapping on his tent and dripping off the trees onto the pine needle–covered ground around him.

'Someone should bottle that sound,' he thought as he nodded off to sleep.

Chapter 11: Boat Ride on Jackson Lake

Dave awoke before sunrise and lay back on top of his sleeping bag with his fingers interlocked behind his head, absorbing how great all of this was. He hadn't read a newspaper, seen a TV, read a stock quote, or surfed the Web in a week. He couldn't honestly say if there was still a world outside of the mountains anymore—and he didn't care.

His thoughts were trying to remember when he last felt this way or this good, and the closest he could recall was the time he went backpacking in Glacier National Park. It seemed like eons ago.

During one of his hikes through the park, he had broken out of some thick woods to discover he was standing on the edge of a cliff. It dropped off into a vast valley of swaying wildflowers of every color. The valley stretched out for miles in front of him. In the foreground was an icy blue glacier lake, with steel-colored, snow-tipped granite glaciers frozen as sentinels in the background.

In the middle of all this on the horizon, a golden setting sun reflected off the lake, with orange-colored beams of light shooting over everything, bathing him in colors and trying to absorb him where he stood. Nothing from the psychedelic '60s ever produced anything with so many lights and different colors.

As he was lying in his tent recalling the trip, he realized that the stress that had been building up in him for months had left him for good. He was thoroughly enjoying how relaxed he felt. Nature's charm was working, but then there was something else he still couldn't put his finger on. The transformation was almost complete.

Dave finally got up and noticed that the other campers were coming out of their tents. Rachel made pancakes, and everyone remarked at how great they were. The plan for today had been decided yesterday, so much of the conversation at the table revolved around it.

While the group had been traveling to the village the previous day, they had crossed the Snake River at a couple of points. It turned out to be not much more than a slow-moving large creek. They were supposed to white water raft down it and were disappointed that the water was so low. Mitch agreed it was too low, and Dave felt better since he was the only one who had wanted to do the rafting.

Since nobody wanted to float down a creek, they tried to come up with an alternate plan. Rachel suggested they go on a boat ride on Jackson Lake that would take them out to the base of the Tetons.

Even Ray, who a few days before swore he would never get in a boat again, agreed to go on the ride.

After the breakfast mess was cleaned up, Rachel announced that Dave was to sit and drink his coffee while everyone else packed up the trailer with the breakfast coolers and their gear.

Dave was in shock. Not that one of his primary responsibilities was removed from him, but that she thought they were capable of such a feat.

She said she was going to go clean up at the restrooms and, by the time she got back, she expected everything to be packed and the campsite to be spotless. He stared at her in disbelief while she shot him a look and told him not to lift a finger.

The rest of the misfit campers got up, and all moved in unison toward the trailer, where all of their gear was strewn about on the ground.

They stared down at their packs and suitcases, then at the trailer, then at each other for a long while.

Mitch said something, and then suddenly Gene took charge by whipping open the trailer door. He flailed his arms and pointed at the different articles while barking out commands.

"You do that one here, you zip up that. Here, that one he throws in now." A better drill sergeant or "Manager of Trailer Loading" had Dave ever met. In less than ten minutes, everything was loaded and the trailer door shut.

"We did it!" Gene shouted with joy. High fives went all around. Dave was in total shock.

Rachel returned and congratulated them all on doing a great job while she helped Dave pick his jaw up off the ground.

"I knew they could do it," she smiled wryly at him. They all jumped in the van and drove down to Colter Bay and parked by the dock.

Rachel bought the tickets for the excursion boat while the rest of the group wandered around the front of the General Store. Since they had a couple of hours to kill, it was time to go shopping again at the gift shop.

Dan stood by the front door looking at and twirling a postcard display. Dave walked around with Gene and kept him busy, or was it the other way around?

The first thing Dave did was get Gene some coffee. At the cashier, after paying for it, he asked Gene, "What do you say"? Instead of saying thank you, he blurted back, "I'm not dopey, you say thank you!" It was as if Dave had insulted him for treating him like a little kid or something. Gene was maturing right before his eyes.

They then bumped into Mitch, who asked Dave to help him pick out some 3D viewing slides. Consequently, with Gene helping out by pointing out different things, and Mitch asking him questions, Dave pretty much felt like a pinball getting bounced back and forth. He finally found everything Mitch wanted, and Gene was excited that he had helped.

After the group gathered together again, they walked down to the lake and sat by the dock to wait for the departure of their boat ride.

The Tetons were on the other side of the lake, and some of the snow-capped mountaintops were obscured by clouds. It was awe-inspiring watching the peaks and their colored moods change as the clouds moved through the mountaintops. Then the sun would break through now and then, revealing a whole, new, unique picture. The time went by too quickly.

Eventually, a guy who appeared to be in his 70s and wearing a captain's hat stopped and asked, "Are you folks waiting for a boat ride?" A chorus of chimed "yeses" rang out from the group.

"Well, I'll be ready in a minute if you want to stand by the entrance to the dock," the captain replied.

That was all Gene needed to hear. He grabbed "Ma's" arm and hurried her to the front, while the rest obligingly tagged along.

After about ten more minutes, the captain appeared again and asked another group if they were waiting for the boat. They said they were, so he told them to join the group at the entrance. The captain then took a space at the dock entrance, faced everyone, and started his announcement.

"I'm Captain Bob, and I will be taking everyone out on the boat." Gene immediately grabbed Bob's hand, started shaking it, and eagerly cried out, "Oh, hi, Bob. I'm Gene, and this is my buddy."

He pointed at Rachel. She started laughing as Captain Bob acknowledged Gene and "his Buddy". Dave wondered if Gene was forgetting genders again and would start calling him "Ma" now.

Captain Bob gave a brief speech about being careful walking out on the dock. Then he told them to go ahead and start loading. Gene dropped Rachel's arm and started skip-hopping out onto the dock imploring everyone to "C'mon" by turning and windmilling his arm.

Gene reached the boat right behind Bob, turned around, and yelled at everyone to "hurry up". Dave was bringing up the rear, trying to conceal his laughter again.

Mitch grabbed a seat next to a window so he could finish the roll of film in his camera. Gene sat by a window next to Rachel, and the rest sat on the long bench seat in the front.

Along with the drone of the engine, Bob was an exceedingly boring Captain as he explained the geography of the Tetons and the lake. Dave slept through most of the trip, as did a few others.

After the boat trip was over and the group disembarked from the boat, they walked back to the van. Most of the group said they liked the ride, but Mitch and Rachel were disappointed that it wasn't a ride down the Snake River.

Rachel announced that the rest of the day was personal time again at the camp. When everyone unloaded at the camp, Todd and Dave took the van back to the village store so Todd could make his phone call again, and Dave could buy some Hershey bars for the s'mores as a dessert that night.

When the two returned to the camp, Dave noticed Rachel was frustrated over the gas stove because it wouldn't stay lit. She had a full pot of spaghetti sauce sitting on the side of it.

After she gave up and Dave did his best to figure out the problem, she dumped out the sauce and it was time to roast hot dogs over the wood fire again. She didn't want to damage the pot over the wood fire.

Strange, Ray didn't want any hot dogs this time, but everyone else roasted their dogs, and ate them with coleslaw and potato salad on the side. The group had a great supper, recalling all the good times they had on the trip.

Later, they all got sticky roasting marshmallows for the s'mores. After it was over and everything was cleaned up, Dave finished stoking the fire with the rest of the wood. The group all sat around the fire, watching as the flames slowly ate away at the wood.

One by one, the tired campers grew sleepy and retired for the night, until it was just Todd, Mitch, and Dave left to watch the dying fire.

They stretched out on the ground, staring up through the pine trees at the Milky Way. Mitch and Dave spent the next hour or so philosophizing about the Bible and whether there was life on other planets. It was determined there wasn't any real life, or perhaps maybe there was pre-Adamic life, but most likely there were creatures of some sort.

Their conclusion resolved that Time and Justice hadn't run their predetermined courses on earth yet though, so all of space hung in limbo waiting. If someone on the outside had heard them talking, he or she would probably be convinced by their conversation that they were completely stoned.

The trio sat in silence for a long time after their deeply thoughtful contemplation of the vastness of the universe and their self-inspired comments. Dave's soul was in the bubble soaring in the Milky Way when Todd broke the silence and hurtled him back to earth. "I wonder if Mike got my postcard yet." It was time for bed.

Dave led his fellow dreamers back to their tent in time to hear Ray snoring like a bear. They thought it would be funny to pretend they were bears also and snore back at Ray, but then they figured the thought was funnier than the action.

Dave crawled into his tent, wishing they could keep doing this for a very long time—just without Ray.

Chapter 12: The Beginning of the Long Journey Back

Dave was sound asleep when he thought he heard someone call his name. Moving from deep sleep to mid-consciousness, he waited to see whether it was his imagination. He was hoping it was because he wanted to go back to his dream.

But no, it was Mary whispering his name again. Struggling to awake himself, he finally managed a half-spoken, "What?" Her next whispering from the other side of his tent door caused him to sit up in alarm in the pitch dark.

"Doris is gone."

He tried, as calmly as possible, to say thank you, and asked her to, "Please go wake up Rachel."

He hurriedly threw on his sweatshirt and pants and burst through the tent door with his flashlight in time to see Rachel wrapping herself in a jacket and stumbling toward his tent.

As they strained to get their wits about them and their eyes adjusted to the darkness, his flashlight lit up his watch—it was almost 5:00 am.

Bundled up to ward off the early morning chill, they decided to first check out the restrooms, do a quick look around the area, then, if they still hadn't found her, to hop in the van and drive around the loop roads.

They raced up the trail to the restrooms hoping to get lucky and see Doris, but no such luck or Doris was found there. Then they ran back down to the campsite. Dave then discovered Doris's flashlight was still in her tent, and so was her jacket. This was not good news.

Mary sat at the table smoking a cigarette. Rachel asked her how long Doris had been gone, but she didn't know.

Dave thought it was strange that Mary was smoking because it was the first time he had seen her with a cigarette. It didn't seem right that grandma should be smoking. The image added to the dreamlike eeriness of the morning.

"Mary, you wait here, and don't tell anyone what happened if they ask," Rachel said hurriedly.

Dave added, "Tell them we are out getting stuff for breakfast, and keep your eye out for Doris too."

Dave and Rachel thanked Mary and then jumped into the van and took off to check out the other campsites. Dave shone his flashlight beam out the window, frantically lighting up the tents, cars, and woods, searching in vain to see Doris shuffling around or sitting somewhere.

"I don't think she would wander off into the woods," Rachel broke the silence. "Maybe she went to the restrooms and got confused on her way back."

"Well, it's cold enough to see our breath, and she doesn't have her jacket on. I just hope she didn't fall and hit her head. Hypothermia could be setting in," Dave replied.

"Don't say that. We'll find her," Rachel quickly answered.

They anxiously searched the local trails, roads, and campsites, but Doris didn't turn up. Then Rachel suggested the next steps.

"Let's go back to camp, check out everyone else's tent—especially Gene's—and then you stay with the rest of the group while I go to the ranger station to form a search party."

He was sort of hoping Doris *did* go into Gene's tent since he had thrown out invitations to her in the previous days, amidst his other rambled phrases.

Whenever Dave caught Gene wooing Doris, he had informed Gene that no one but Dan would be in his tent with him. Gene would continue on in his ramblings as if nothing had happened. This further induced Dave's- Gene-as-conman theory.

Rachel made the last turn that would bring them back to camp. As they were turning into the campsite, the headlights first shone on Mary and her red-colored rain suit, then with her arms folded, looking down and walking in circles—Doris.

"There she is…" they both sighed at the same time.

Rachel slammed the van into Park, jumped out, and hurried over to hug her while Dave threw Doris's jacket over her. Doris didn't seem at all concerned and was confused by all the attention. She said she made a wrong turn coming out of the restroom and had been walking around the roads trying to find the campsite. They must have just missed her.

Dave and Doris walked back up to her tent to get her flashlight.

"I think my zipper is stuck on my jacket," she told Dave.

"Okay, I'll see if I can fix it once we find your flashlight," Dave replied.

Standing beside her tent now, while Doris held the flashlight, he was trying to help her get the zipper unstuck when they both heard a rustling in the woods behind them.

Dave quickly grabbed the flashlight from her hands, fully expecting to see the shape of a bear coming toward them. It was a bear, all right—a human bear. Mitch was stumbling and breaking his way out of the woods.

"Mitch! What are you doing in the woods?" Dave asked, dumbfounded and louder than intended..

Half laughing, Mitch stammered, "I must have gotten turned around."

Dave looked up at the sky and cried out, "What is it with you guys? Did you think Rachel and I were bored or something?" They all started laughing in relief.

It was still dark when they walked back down toward the picnic tables. Dave found Rachel pulling the breakfast coolers out of the trailer.

"I might as well start breakfast since I'm fully awake," she told him.

"I was fixing the zipper on Doris's jacket, and Mitch came stumbling out of the woods and scared the crap out of us," Dave replied back.

She sat on the end of the trailer pleading, "Why are they doing this to us now?"

"I don't know… maybe they're on an adventure or something? I need to go to the restrooms," Dave mumbled as he took off up the trail.

By the time he returned, the women and Mitch had the table set up for breakfast. The stove still wouldn't start, so they would have to wait until they stopped at the General Store for coffee. They both definitely wanted coffee this morning.

The rest of the gang eventually awoke, and the cereal buffet was presented again. Gene was confused over why he couldn't have his coffee, and Dan pointed to the sad face in his book.

While they were slurping down the breakfast, for some reason, Gene started pointing at the group sitting around the table, giggling. Then he broke out in guffawing laughter and couldn't quit. It was infectious, and the entire group all laughed uncontrollably.

Dave didn't know why Gene started laughing or why everyone else joined in. Maybe it was a relief reaction, and they were all somewhat glad the ordeal part of the trip was over. Dave determined it was just one of those things that will be stored away somewhere and will have to remain a mystery until all things are revealed at the end of the age.

The now well-traveled campers managed to get the tents down and all the gear loaded in record time. The fact that it had started raining again might have had something to do with it.

It was Dave's turn to drive now, on the long journey back home. He hopped behind the steering wheel to turn the van around, but the engine made a sickening "click" sound when he turned the key—the battery was dead again.

This made little sense to him. Why would the battery intermittently go dead? The only thing he could think of was that it had something to do with the rain. But it had started on other days when it had been raining.

Rachel volunteered to hike over to one of the other campsites while Dave dug out the jumper cables and raised the hood.

By the time he got the hood up, she returned with a guy from the next campsite with his pickup truck. He looked like a middle-aged hippie wannabe, with long straggly hair, a beard, and a red bandanna tied around his forehead.

The truck's engine was missing badly, and Dave wasn't sure the guy could keep his truck running long enough to jump the van, but he did.

The guy jumped back in his truck and drove off before Dave could thank him or offer him any money. He finally got the van backed up to the trailer. Rachel asked if he could get the trailer on by himself, and Dave replied, "Pretty sure, Ma."

The trailer slipped on without a problem, and then Dave continued his Gene imitation with Rachel, "You got coffee?"

They both laughed as they jumped in the van. Rachel checked to make sure everyone was aboard and buckled up, and then the van roared down the road to the General Store. They were the only ones at the store, so it didn't take Rachel long at all to get the drinks.

Dave jumped out of the van to help her bring coffee and hot chocolate out for everyone. The drinks quickly warmed up everyone's rain-chilled bodies, and one and all remarked at how good the hot drinks tasted.

It rained all the way out of the Tetons and quit sometime before they drove into Grant Village in Yellowstone. This was where they were going to drop off Mary to meet her caregivers.

Dave pulled into the parking lot in the back of the lodge and jumped out to get Mary's gear from the trailer. In the meantime, Rachel helped everyone else out of the van, and by the time Dave found Mary's gear and placed it on the sidewalk, the group was huddled around Rachel outside the van.

Dave walked up to them to see what they were looking at, and they all turned around with smiles on their faces. Rachel was holding a cake roll with a lit candle in the middle. They sang happy birthday to Dave, and he pretended he was the choir director.

Although it wasn't his birthday for a few more days, Mary had found out from Rachel when his birthday was while they had been off getting ice cream bars a few days back. Mary collaborated with Rachel to celebrate the event before she left. *'Sweet old grandma',* Dave thought.

They all sang happy birthday to Gene too, because he kept saying it was his birthday. Unfortunately, the party soon ended, and Mary's group still hadn't shown up. Rachel went to the front desk and was told that Mary's group had called and would be late.

"We will be happy to keep an eye on her," the manager told Rachel. They waited as long as possible for someone to pick her up, but finally had to leave her at the lodge with the management in charge of her.

Mary had complained only once the whole time on the trip—the chili had been too spicy—but, other than that, Dave thought she had really a good time, and he hoped he was right.

It was raining again as they drove the rest of the way through Yellowstone. It finally quit just before they drove into Cody. Doris picked a chicken place to have lunch. They found a crowded combo Mexican and chicken restaurant on the other side of town.

Everyone gave his or her order to Rachel and she passed them on to the cashier. Gene and Dan wanted coffee, but the pot was empty at the moment.

"We will let you know when we have some more ready," the gal behind the counter told Gene and Dan. Gene had a pout formed on his face as he walked out to where Dave was setting up tables.

"They don't have any coffee here," Gene tried to tell his sad tale.

"I think they are just out for the moment, Gene," Dave told him while smiling at Gene's sad face.

The rest of the gang joined them and sat at the tables. The cook screwed up the order, so Rachel had to go through each one to make sure each person got what he or she had ordered. Gene was bugging Rachel for his coffee throughout the sorting. Dan was also constantly pointing to his coffee cup picture.

Dave thought up a great idea.

"Since the restaurant gave us such lousy service, why not send Gene up to see if the coffee is ready yet—that should be really interesting." Dave slyly smiled at Rachel.

She thought it was a great idea too, and told Gene to go ask for his coffee. That was all he needed to hear.

Gene barged his way through to the front of the line of people. He waved his arms and yelled until he got somebody's attention. Then he blurted out to the unfortunate restaurant worker, "Oh, hi, you got coffee? I need coffee." The gal looked put out, but went to get his coffee. All the while, Gene was going through his auto-phrases with her. Rachel and Dave were almost on the floor laughing.

Although the woman gave Gene his coffee, he still relentlessly pestered her, and a frown began to spread across her face. Rachel figured she should go rescue her, as Dave was still out of commission.

When Rachel got to Gene, he was asking the gal, "Are you happy?" Then Rachel lost it again and laughed uncontrollably. Gene said he needed water because the coffee was too hot, and he started crooning his Country Western cool water song to her. Dave had tears streaming down his face by the time he got coffee for Dan, and Rachel wasn't much better, as she barely made it back to the booth.

When lunch was finally over, Dave drove back to Ten Sleeps canyon while Rachel started working on the client evaluations, which were part of her trip report. She was required to answer a questionnaire on each person, describing how well he or she had adjusted to new environments physically, emotionally, and if the client had taken part in the group activities.

In addition, she was asked to document if the client had experienced any problems. She was to point out what the client did well and not so well, and any newly learned skills.

Finally, she was to indicate if she thought the client would enjoy any other trips. She asked Dave for his input on each person because he had done performance reviews in the past, and she thought he could provide decent, objective viewpoints.

They pulled into the same campsite in Ten Sleeps they'd had before and were able to set up the tents much quicker this time. Rachel told everyone that they were going out to a restaurant for supper, but not before everyone had a shower. Nobody had taken one since they'd been there before.

Ray said he wasn't taking a shower, and Rachel quickly remarked back at him that he was taking a shower. He blew up again, but Rachel held her ground, stating that if he didn't, he would sit in the van while they all ate.

Bad Attitude plodded back and forth at the picnic table for a few minutes, miserably contemplating his choices, and then decided he would go take a shower if Dave showed him how.

Everyone else could shower on their own now, and Ray was cordial to Dave while he showed him where to put his clothes and stuff. Dave started the shower for him. Gene then walked in, and Dave got him started too, since it was getting late.

Gene asked Dave to hold his wallet and change, and told him not to steal it. Dave laughed and told him he didn't steal coffee money. It was the wrong choice of words, because Gene started in with, "You got coffee?" followed by a few other auto-phrases.

Gene stopped himself and showed Dave a picture of "the Baby" out of his wallet. It was an old family picture with the dad holding a baby. Gene informed him, "… the baby is mine, and I go there at Christmas." Dave figured the people must be relatives who invited him over for Christmas.

It was the only picture Gene had, but he sure liked the baby. Could it be Gene? Dave asked him, but Gene did not give him a discernible answer.

In the meantime, Ray finished his shower and couldn't wait to leave the building while Gene was in there. Gene continued with pulling clothes out of his suitcase, showing Dave all the items he had bought at his local discount department stores. Dave finally got Gene into the shower and told him he would stop back later after he found his toothbrush.

"Okay, Buddy," Gene quickly replied. Dave guessed he was Gene's buddy again, and was glad he wasn't "Ma."

Dave sat down with Rachel at the picnic table.

"I think Gene is highly trainable just from what he's learned in the past eight days. What did they do in the institutions for the past forty-two years?" Dave asked Rachel.

"It may have taken them that long just to get him to the learning capabilities he now has," she told him.

"Well, if he was given more one-on-one attention, he might be put into society without as much supervision," Dave remarked.

"Perhaps, but some old institutions didn't provide much training or teaching. They mainly kept their patients docile and drugged and away from society. He probably learned what he knows now from his personal caregivers," she answered him again.

'What a waste,' Dave thought as his transformation was taking its final hold.

Just then he heard Gene yell, "Ma!" Dave turned to see Gene standing in front of the restroom/shower door in all of his glory.

"Gene!" Dave shouted. "Get back in there and put some clothes on." As he jumped up from the table and ran toward the shower building, he glanced around to see if any other campers had seen Gene. There wasn't anyone outside at the moment, but that didn't mean nobody saw him.

'Ach—cheap entertainment,' he thought. And so much for letting him loose in society.

Dave waved at Gene to get back inside, and Gene argued back at him. Dave got him back inside the door, but never figured out what the problem was. Gene was trying to tell him something about his clothes bag, but his words were unintelligible.

Dave took his quick shower and waited inside the shower room with Gene until he finished dressing. Everybody else waited for them at the picnic tables. Then the whole group climbed in the van to go eat supper. Dave drove back into a town to a restaurant they had spotted on the way through to Ten Sleeps.

They got to the restaurant and everyone sat down and ordered just before the restaurant closed. The waitresses and management were extremely hospitable, even though they had to clean up around the vacationers while they ate. The food was great, and it pretty much set everyone up for an early–to-bed night.

When they got back, they all hit their sleeping bags, because it was going to be another early rising the next morning for the long drive to Chamberlain, the final campsite on the trip. It had been a really long day, and Dave slept like a rock until the next morning.

Chapter 13: Chamberlain

Dave awoke before anyone else did and woke Rachel. "I'm going to grab a quick shower," he told her.

"Okay," she drowsily answered back. "Thanks for waking me." He wasn't sure if she said it sarcastically or not.

The rest all rustled out of their tents later on. They finished polishing off the cereals, and Dan finished up the other leftovers.

It was routine now, getting everyone cleaned up, everything torn down, rolled up, or stuffed in, and packed up. Ray helped a little, but at least he dealt with his own gear.

They all piled into the van and stopped at the convenience store in town to get everyone coffee or hot chocolate.

As they drove through Bighorn Pass, Rachel enjoyed the scenery; she hadn't gotten to see much of it coming through the other way.

Dave thought it was great when he finally got back on the freeway again, and he put the pedal down, put a tape in the tape deck, and did his best to eliminate as many miles as possible to Chamberlain.

They stopped once for gas, and the owner gave them all free coffee or hot chocolate. Gene thought the white-bearded guy was Santa Claus, but asked him why he put his coffee into a "dopey" cup. Apparently, if it wasn't a souvenir mug and just a Styrofoam cup, it was a dopey cup.

They also stopped for lunch at a restaurant that Rachel spotted in a small town. It was actually Dan's choice—he had pointed out a restaurant image to her the previous day in his book. The food was average, but it gave Rachel and Dave a chance to work on her reports again.

Later on that afternoon, Dave had to stop at a roadside rest stop to give his eyes a break. While everyone else went to the restrooms, he lay out on a grassy bank and let the warm sun shine on him. He was fully content to rest there for eternity. However, eternity soon ended when Todd woke him up from his power nap. "I wonder if Mike knows about the fire."

Chamberlain sat on the banks of the Missouri River. There was an old campground there that the army used at one time. The old barracks had been remodeled and were now used for large groups of visitors.

Huge oak trees separated nice campsites along the river, but there were lots of mosquitoes. The campers sprayed themselves down with repellent, quickly put up the tents, and zippered them up to keep the bugs out.

Gene decided on a pizza place for supper, and everyone chose his or her own toppings. Ray just wanted cheese.

Ray's attitude had improved immensely during the day. He even tried to joke with the group on a couple of occasions and made feeble attempts at helping out.

They were so used to seeing him scowl all the time. It actually looked as if it hurt him to smile even the slightest smile. It appeared as if he was straining unused muscles in his face to raise the invisible lead weights that held down the corners of his mouth.

Rachel thought he figured out she was doing reports on him and now he was trying to gain her good graces. It didn't work.

Because of the notes in her report about his inability to get along with anyone, he would never go on any trip with her again.

When they finished the pizzas, the group returned to their site, and Dave started a campfire. Everyone tried to sit out by the fire for a while and watch the river flow by, but the bugs were too annoying. Rachel told everyone it was okay to go back into the tents.

Dave tried sitting by the fire for a few more moments, but was driven into his tent as well. Rachel said she could stand it for a while longer.

He caught up in his journal and was lying out on his sleeping bag when he heard several excited voices outside his tent. He peered out through the tent flap to see what was going on. Coming toward him was what appeared to be a coal miner with mosquito netting over her face. It was Rachel with a miner's light strapped to a baseball cap on her forehead. She was carrying a tray of freshly made chocolate chip cookies.

Dave grabbed a couple off of her tray.

"How could you do this?" He was astounded that she could do such a thing for the group.

"Ah, it's nuthin'," she said, mimicking Doris. He could tell that her smile behind the netting was brighter than the light on her forehead.

He quickly polished off the cookies and fell asleep listening to the hum of mosquitoes, the rapids in the river, and the worn-out vacationers softly talking in their tents.

Chapter 14: Last day-Back Home Again

Dave woke Rachel to tell her he would be in the shower. "Thanks," she said sleepily. "I wanted to get an early start again today since I have to be back to the office and leave on another trip at 6:00 this evening."

"Man, how do you do it?" he asked her.

"I love it, that's how," she emphatically told him.

As the sun rose in a deep blue sky, everybody got cleaned up and the gear packed and stowed in the trailer as if they were as regimented as the army who used to stay there.

It was to-go breakfast for everyone at a fast-food restaurant, followed by Dave putting the pedal down again on the freeway.

The first stop was at the small airport to drop Mitch off. The rest of the group said their goodbyes, and then Dave took everyone else through the restrooms while Rachel and Mitch secured his ticket and connection through his connecting airport.

Mitch had given Dave his e-mail address during the trip, and Dave had assured him he would keep in touch. Dave thought he would remember Mitch for the rest of his life. The man had definitely left an impression on him with his ability to handle incredible obstacles each and every day without complaint.

"Mitch, if the opportunity ever arises, I will certainly travel with you again—anywhere, anytime. You've taught me a lot."

"I have?" Mitch smiled. "Thanks, I had fun." And he stuck his hand out for Dave to shake. Dave was truly sorry to see him go.

Everyone climbed back into the van and they all claimed they were excited about going home. Although they were now almost back home, Rachel decided to stop once more for an early dinner, not sure the clients would get fed again until the next day.

Doris and Todd picked a hamburger place, and when they arrived, Gene thought he would scrape his tennis shoes all the way through the restaurant making chirping sounds on the freshly waxed floors. He just smiled and said, "Birds," to anyone who would listen.

The cashier was giving Rachel a hard time stating they couldn't pack the to-go food in a separate bag for each person.

"Would you like the group to come up and give their order personally and separately to you?" Rachel inquired almost sarcastically. The cashier gave the group the once-over and decided she could figure out how to package the orders separately. The Misfit Campers from the Loony Bin had struck again!

Rachel had phoned ahead to the office the previous day at the rest stop to see if she could bring Gene to the office instead of his airport. The itinerary had them dropping him at the airport around 3:00 pm, and his flight wasn't until 8:00 pm. She did not feel good about this at all.

She wanted to take him with her to the airport when she left on her next trip, since she had to pick up someone there, anyway. The company eventually agreed to the plan.

Apparently, neither Gene's group home nor the company thought it was a big deal to leave him at the airport on his own for five hours. Dave realized now that there is still a lot of work to be done in this field of work, or at least getting the right people to work in it. Of course, when a person can make more money delivering pizzas, it is difficult to get the right people.

They pulled up to Stretching Horizons at around 4:00 pm. Rachel brought everyone into the office, and Dave checked to see if his truck was still there in one piece—it was.

One guy from India came out and helped Dave unload the trailer and bring the gear inside. Gene wanted to help too, but there was a bee bothering him, so he went back into the office. Dave teased him, pretending to be a bee that was trying to sting him.

"You pickin on me. Cut dat out."

Dave looked out the front office window in time to see Dan drive off with his caregiver. It was the first time in ten days that Dan did not have a big beaming smile on his face. It sent a weird shudder through his heart, and he felt sorry that he had not had a chance to say good-bye.

Ray came over and stuck his hand out. Dave remembered Ray had not shaken his hand when he'd presented it at the beginning of the trip, and wondered for a moment if he should return the favor.

Dave wasn't sure what it meant coming from Ray, but he took his limp hand and shook it. Then Ray turned away and went back to grumbling to himself.

Dave found Gene again and told him he was leaving and how much he really enjoyed camping with him. He didn't think it registered with Gene that they probably would never see each other again.

Dave said goodbye to everyone else, told Rachel to call when she got back, loaded up his truck, and drove off. He stopped at a coffee shop to reflect on the trip and make his last entries into his journal.

He chuckled in his mind, remembering what Rachel had written in their evaluation of Gene. She pointed out that Gene stole the coffee mug, accosted females, and perhaps his tent mate, and farted in public. Then they both commented that they would enjoy having him on a trip with them again. What would the people who read this evaluation think of them as camping guides?

During the past ten days, Dave had exorcised his own character-flawed demons. He had learned there was value in people—even within his own developmentally challenged self. It wasn't simply the people themselves that had transformed him. It was the interaction with people of special needs that had broken him out of his self-induced prison and had taught him to celebrate other people's lives.

He then reconsidered for a moment, the thought he'd had at the beginning of the trip that it wouldn't be such a terrible life if he took the leap into the abyss of the "state-supported happy place". He could get himself a picture book, fart like a chain saw, sneak gropes on women in public, ask endless questions, and get away with it all!

Nah! He thoughtfully reconsidered again. He would wait and do all those things in his old age, anyway. He was ready to go on another trip with Rachel, or even get more involved with those of special needs. After all, he was now a full-fledged, Alien Camping Misfit in a Crystalline Bubble.

Acknowledgments

Much improvement has been accomplished in group homes and with their staff since the inspired events in this book took place. However, more work still needs to be done.

It was not the intent to denigrate any work that these wonderful people perform. The desire was to inspire others to get involved in the betterment of the lives of those with special needs. It is doubtful there is anything as equally rewarding in this life as working with the developmentally disabled.

Mr. Nordstrom is also the author of:

"The Revelation Happened". ISBN-13 : 978-0578955339

He is retired and engages in freelance writing in his spare time, and is a Texas Tech Raider's fan.

A portion of the author's profits from this book will go to assist organizations involved in helping those with special needs.

Email: TheDesertPG@protonmail.com